LARP

The Battle for Verona

by

Justin Calderone

Published Internationally by 42nd Street Publishing Inc.
Pittsburgh, PA

DEDICATION

Thank you:

To my incredible wife Emily, who helped me develop this story, and was a sounding board throughout the process. As each day passes, you become a greater blessing.

To Tara Clapper (tarawrites.com) for doing the first edit of this novel, and for all of your LARP info. You are a bottomless pit of geekness.

To the LARPers on Washington Blvd., for your inspiration. Keep practicing, because you never know.

This book is proof that Jesus keeps His promises (Genesis 50:20) (Malachi 3:10) (Romans 5:3-5)

For dad, grandpa and grandma

PRAISE FOR

LARP

THE BATTLE FOR VERONA

"Justin Calderone's **LARP: The Battle for Verona** is a witty, action-packed adventure that will leave you breathless. Sharp-edged, and lots of fun!" - Jonathan Maberry, multiple Bram Stoker Award winner, and New York Times bestselling author of Assassin's Code and Dust & Decay

"Justin Calderone's **LARP: The Battle for Verona** is a sly parable about the psychic cost of arrested development. It will feel depressingly familiar to anyone already living a life of quiet desperation. It is a tale that cuts across the passivity of modern life, drawing both blood and laughter at times. Imagine "The Ring of the Nibelungs" only with nerds vs. medieval-minded savages. Prepare to be challenged."-Tony Norman, Pittsburgh Post-Gazette

"A Geek Gem. The characters are like real people; they're not tools for satire. Calderone moves the main plot along quickly enough to hold interest and make the action feel intense. There's a fair balance of action, adventure, cynicism, and romance. I would recommend this book for adults and teens."--Fantascize.com

"Justin Calderone populates the narrative with a collection of characters that readers can both relate and care about, ultimately making the novel entertaining as well as appealing."- geekpittsburgh.com

LARP
<u>THE BATTLE FOR VERONA</u>

CHAPTER 1

Sir Den-gar stood at the top of the ravine, surveying the landscape that he had viewed on so many previous mornings. The bright sun shone upon the meadow, illuminating the droplets of dew on the grass, as if liquid silver had rained down during the night.

Den-gar turned his face up to the glowing warmth; his armor sparkled like a million cut diamonds. Surely, the luminescence of his armor was the result of The King's blessing he had received at the previous night's feast.

Off in the distance, the waking sounds of the Kingdom of Verona brought a smile to Sir Den-gar's face. He could hear goats, dogs and horses, people buying, selling and trading. The shouts of "Chickens, two for a pound" made him think of the days when chicken was all he could afford to eat.

Again, Den-gar's gaze swept over the hills and valleys that spread out before him. How often, as a child, his loving grandfather would chase him through those very pastures. After their play, Den-gar's grandfather, the legendary knight Sir Samuel the Wise, would regale young Den-gar with tales of his noble conquests.

Verona was part of Den-gar's fiber, part of his being. He took great pride in his magnificent Kingdom, and it was his honor to protect it. He would kill—or die—for Verona. It was as simple as that.

From the corner of his eye, a plume of black smoke swam into his vision, crashing his daydream. The haze sharpened back to reality, as Den-gar spotted an enemy campground. The adversary, a godless people from the nearby kingdom of Brad, huddled near the stream, their horses drinking from its waters.

Den-gar's jaw clenched, and his gaze leveled on their location. Soon, those crystal clear waters would be polluted with blood. It would not be Den-gar's blood or that of his countrymen. It would be the blood of the enemy, as it had been so many times before.

The ravine marked the point of no return for any army seeking to invade Den-gar's fair Kingdom of Verona. Because of the lush foliage and maze of trees, it took hours for any army to safely navigate the terrain. Den-gar's skilled warriors, trained to navigate and battle in the rough surroundings, scouted the ravine several times each day. Any army that lost its nerve and decided to retreat would be hunted down by Den-gar's heroic battalion.

The side of the ravine closest to Verona was cleared of all foliage. The open field allowed Den-gar's army to quickly descend into the ravine and annihilate any militia foolish enough to invade Verona.

But, if an invading army was not spotted by a guard, the foe could easily climb the hill, and attack Verona.

That had never happened.

Verona's adversaries knew better than to mount an offensive on Den-gar's watch.

Chatting, as their horses gulped Verona's water, the five poorly armed men assumed their presence had gone unnoticed. Their lack of awareness proved them to be scouts. Den-gar felt a fire of rage, hotter than Hades, burning within his chest.

How dare such a lowly army think that they could take mighty Verona?

Did they not know of his reputation?

These men would pay with their miserable lives. Den-gar would slice their heads in two, and pour their cowardly blood into the river, where it would flow back to their enemy village. By his feared name, they would know his wrath.

Den-gar would not return to Verona to summon his men. These feeble scouts needed to be taught a lesson, and a message needed to be sent.

Now.

Drawing his enormous sword, "Leviathan," Den-gar let out a battle cry of "VICTORY" and, as if possessed by the pride of his royal ancestors, charged down the ravine toward the enemy. Their death was a foregone conclusion.

And then the phone rang.

The haze sharpened, into a suburban reality. The open expanse of the rolling hills melted away, and Den-gar, or Dennis, as he was known most of the time, returned to his undersized, fenced-in backyard.

Dennis thoughtlessly dropped his fake sword, and then angrily realized doing so was a really bad idea. Quickly picking up the weapon, Dennis slipped it under his arm, and fished his phone from the pocket of his breeches.

"What are you doing?" It was Brad. Dennis had expected the call, and wasn't looking forward to it.

"Nothing."

"Okay, let me guess," Brad continued, "you've got three watermelons stacked on milk crates in your backyard. You're wearing the 'armor' that you bought from some wacko on the Internet, and you're about to charge the evil watermelons with your foam sword. Am I right? Am I close?"

"They're cantaloupes, and the only thing you're close to is me hanging up on you." Dennis's light brown eyebrows furrowed, and the blue of his eyes intensified as Brad spoke again.

"So you're practicing for the annual dorkfest in Uniontown, right? Are you really going to Uniontown again? I mean, seriously, you've been doing this for years. You've gotta be tired of running up and down a field all day with a toy sword and a rubber shield."

Dennis could feel Brad's broad, smart-aleck smile through the phone.

"Yes, I'm really going to Uniontown," Dennis replied, agitated. "Are you really going to keep asking me that every year?"

"If you would stop going," Brad replied, attempting to sound logical, "then maybe I would stop asking."

"Every time I talk to you, I lose a few points off my IQ," Dennis shot back.

Silence.

Dennis pointed his sword at the cantaloupes, examining it

for cracks. The Den-gar part of his brain was encouraging him to go inside, and begin a sword and shield demonstration on Brad's beloved trophy case.

"I just don't understand it. Why do you need to keep hanging out with those LARD weirdoes?"

"It's LARP . . . Live Action Role Playing." Years of frustration oozed out of Dennis's usually calm voice. "And I do it because it makes me happy. Somebody wins, somebody loses, and everyone has fun."

"But how can someone win, when everyone there is a loser? Explain that one, Mr. Magna Cum Laude college man!" Brad laughed.

Dennis subconsciously squeezed the handle of his sword, as if preparing to strike.

"Like your hobby is any better. Every weekend you and your high school meathead buddies head out and play football like you're still in high school. So your weekend reality isn't much different than mine, is it?"

Dennis could feel Brad's frustration over the phone. It was Brad's fault for calling in the first place. A smile crept across Dennis's mouth.

"Yeah, well," Brad said, retreating, "If I wouldn't have blown out my knees, I would have been a freshman starter at any Big 10 school in the country." Dennis rolled his eyes. He'd been hearing that same excuse for years. When push came to shove, Brad always relied on his bum knees.

"You live your reality, I'll live mine. I'll talk to you when I get back." Dennis punched the red END button, silencing Brad, at least for the time being.

Dennis paused, and took a deep breath. His chest pounded as his nasal passages cleared. Brad's words, and laugh, played in an irritating loop in his head, as he blamed himself for answering the call.

The phone rang again.

"I told you I don't want to talk to you until I get back!" Dennis roared, almost hoping for another confrontation.

"What are you talking about? Don't tell me you took a

header down the hill in your backyard while you were training! The last thing we need this weekend is for Sir Den-gar to have a concussion." It was Mark.

"Oh, sorry, man," Dennis said, regaining his composure. "I didn't look at the caller ID before I answered."

"No problem," Mark said. "So . . . guess you just hung up with Brad, huh?"

"Yeah." Dennis shook his head in disgust.

"You oughta be used to it by now. In fact, after all these years, you should even expect it. That knuckle-dragger brother of yours is nothing if not predictable," Mark replied.

"It doesn't get any less irritating, though. I don't know why he doesn't leave me alone about it." Dennis sighed.

"His opinion doesn't matter, and neither does he," Mark said confidently, trying to support his friend. "Not that I don't feel your pain, but we gotta talk shop. Or LARP, as it is. Is Jen coming this weekend? Please say 'yes', please say 'yes', please say 'yes'."

"She didn't want me to say anything—"

"Yes!!!" Mark exclaimed. Dennis could hear him jumping up and down. "Once we decimate Oakmont, I will proceed to weave the fair Jennifer into my web of love."

Dennis laughed. "You gotta give it up. She's not interested."

"Yes, she is," Mark said. "She just doesn't know it yet. I'm telling you, I can smell her pheromones from here. She's . . . she's the one who's after me, really."

"You're the one with the concussion, not me," Dennis quipped. "Look, I gotta go finish packing. Freddy and I will be over later to pick you up."

"Right. Tell Jen I can feel her essence . . . her very soul . . . and will be with her soon," Mark responded, dramatically.

Dennis hung up the phone, exhaled in disbelief, and headed for his bedroom. He lived in a modest, ranch-style house that had been in his family for three generations. After his parents retired to Arizona, Dennis turned their bedroom into his LARP storage room. The oak closets throughout the room guarded his weapons and suits of hybrid polyurethane armor. Dennis searched the sturdy closets, trying to choose the right suit for the upcoming tournament in Uniontown.

The black scratch on his brown body armor was still there from three years ago. It happened during the battle at Rosedale. Freddy had been cornered and badly outnumbered by a gang of warlocks.

Until Sir Den-gar appeared.

The warlocks had their backs to him and didn't see him coming until it was too late. As he boldly approached, Dennis could see Freddy's smile. The other team probably had no idea why Freddy was smiling. Freddy was about to meet his doom. Had he gone mad? But Freddy knew that when Sir- Den-gar appeared, it was the enemy who was outnumbered.

The warlocks could have been slaughtered before they knew what hit them. But that's not how Sir Den-gar liked his victories. Plus, it was more fun to battle than to ambush.

Sir Den-gar gave a playful whistle, and the three enemies turned to see him and Leviathan waiting to wipe them from the face of the earth.

As they charged Den-gar, Freddy removed his dagger and buried it in the back of a warlock. Den-gar dropped to the ground, cutting several warlocks off at the knees, while quickly rising to plunge Leviathan into the others' chests.

Dennis opened another memory-filled closet, to examine his favorite suit. Normally, polyurethane was incredibly durable, but it had shredded like paper during the battle in Scenic Heights. Mark had been in trouble, again, his spells just a nonsensical diatribe. The ogre he was battling wasn't in the mood for Mark's pompous attitude, and was about to hang him from a tree, upside-down, via his robe.

Den-gar had been nearby and saw what was developing. He was tempted to let the events run their natural course, as Mark probably deserved his fate. Luckily for Mark, loyalty and team spirit prevailed. Den-gar quickly disposed of his opponent, and sprinted over to help Mark.

The enormous ogre heard Den-gar coming and easily pushed him aside. Den-gar crashed to the ground, his armor ripping on a rock. All he could do was watch the ogre hang Mark from the tree. The ogre walked away, laughing.

Dennis stood up, and, in frustration, examined his damaged armor.

Mark, upside-down, scolded, "See, it ripped! I told you not to buy your armor from Slovenia! Everyone knows they make the worst polyurethane on the planet. They're still in the Dark Ages when it comes to replica battle armor!"

Dennis shook his head, and walked away. He still didn't know how Mark got out of the tree that day.

Dennis walked across the narrow hallway to Brad's old room. The room was just as Brad had left it. A shrine to himself. Dirty, game-used football jerseys hung from the walls, and sparkling trophies littered every surface. When Brad lived at home, he polished them on a weekly basis. Brad had moved out several years ago, yet the trophies continued to shine. Dennis often wondered if Brad snuck in to polish the trophies when he was out. That's something Brad would do, if for no other reason than to remind Dennis of how great he was. Or used to be.

On Brad's nightstand was a stack of autographed pictures. Each picture was signed the same; Stay tough! The Brad. Brad would refer to himself as "The Brad", often saying, "Lots of people are called 'The man', but there's only one Brad, and that's me. I am, 'The Brad'."

Brad was Verona's big hope. A hometown kid who would finally make it big. But his utopian future became a nightmare. Brad injured his knees during a game in his senior year. The joints were permanently damaged, ending his football career. His scholarships evaporated, along with the hope of ever getting out of Verona. Over the years, Brad had become good at hiding his limp. Unless he drank too much, then it reappeared, which tended to happen a lot as he enjoyed frequenting Verona's popular hang-out, The Rivertowne Inn, and reminiscing about his glory days.

Brad did two years at a local community college, and worked as the assistant night manager at Big Ralph's Pre-Owned Car Ranch. Although still a local celebrity—the TV commercials for Big Ralph's featured Brad wearing his faded high school football jersey, saying, "Tell them The Brad sent you!"—His big dream had been reduced to a thirty-second TV spot.

On Brad's dresser were several copies of Sport America's Swimsuit Issue. The cover girl was Brad's high school girlfriend, who, on the defining night of Brad's life, the night of his injury, left the football field with the new starting quarterback.

The front door slammed and a familiar voice reminded Dennis that he needed to finish packing.

"Dennis? You up there?"

"Yeah, up here!" Dennis turned off the light in Brad's room. A small, wiry figure filled the doorway. It was Freddy, Dennis's LARP teammate, and lifelong friend. Dennis and Freddy never bothered ringing the doorbell, or knocking, when they visited each other's houses. They just walked in.

Freddy met Dennis at the entrance to Brad's room. "What are you doing?" Freddy asked.

"Nothing, just packing for this weekend," Dennis answered, trying to conceal his presence in Brad's room.

"Packing in Brad's room?" Freddy replied, honing in on Dennis's discomfort.

Dennis stood silent. Freddy knew the answer.

"C'mon, man. Forget what he says. Believe it or not, Brad is probably jealous of you."

"Look at all this," Dennis said, flipping the light back on. "Why would he be jealous of me?"

Freddy grabbed his friend's arm and led him into the other bedroom. "Why wouldn't he be jealous of you?" On Dennis's walls hung his undergraduate and graduate school diplomas, with Magna Cum Laude stamped on both. In his closet were a dozen suits. The smell of the leather from several pairs of dress shoes filled the air as Freddy opened the closet. Dennis's briefcase, with a company laptop, sat next to his shoes.

"You are a success. Dennis. You're the IT manager at the Bank of Verona, and you've got a lot of professional responsibility for someone your age. Or any age, really. Brad was a success back in high school—not now, when it counts. His glory days have come and gone. That's why he gives you such a hard time."

The truth of Freddy's words sunk in. The physical evidence was all around them, but Dennis still felt like Brad's dorky little brother, just like he did back in high school. It was a feeling he couldn't shake. LARPing was as much proof of that as the fact that he didn't have a girlfriend. "I really don't want to talk about this in front of Mark, because you know how he is. But—"

"You're thinking of quitting LARP," Freddy finished.

Dennis nodded. Freddy knew him so well. "I mean, look at all this stuff." Dennis indicated his armor and LARP gear. "I—we've—spent so much time and money on all of this, and what do we have to show for it?"

"Oh, geez, I don't know. Only ten years of memories and friendship, I guess," Freddy replied, a bit indignant.

"That's . . . that's not what I mean," Dennis stammered, trying to soothe his friend's ego. "It's just that . . . I feel like I've missed out on some things, normal non-LARP things, in the time I've spent running through the woods with a fiberglass sword." He stopped, not wanting to continue, but it had to come out. "Do you remember Alyssa?"

Of course Freddy remembered her. She was Dennis's sort of girlfriend in high school. Alyssa was unforgettable.

"I still think about her," Dennis continued. "Do you know where she is now? She's a TV news reporter in Pittsburgh. Look her up online. She still looks fantastic. I can't help but wonder what would have happened if I hadn't stood her up senior year on Amusement Park Day, so that I could go to some LARP event that I don't even remember. Maybe I'd be living in Pittsburgh now. With her."

"Or," Freddy said, sagely, "maybe you would have split up once she left for college that summer, and you'd be standing right here, anyway."

Dennis looked away. "Still, I would have liked to have had the opportunity. I just feel so trapped right now, by Brad, by Verona, by LARP . . ."

"Look, you're not trapped by anything," Freddy retorted,

trying to salvage the upcoming weekend. "I promise that there won't be any hard feelings from me if you decide to quit, but I really need you to be Sir Den-gar, just one more time, this weekend at Uniontown. After that, we'll talk. Okay?"

"Yeah, okay, fine," Dennis said. "You'll have Den-gar this weekend." He wanted to change topics. Thinking of the weekend reminded Dennis that he would have to deal with LARP. And Mark. Bad combination. "So how's your dad? I haven't seen him at the Rivertowne in a while," he said, continuing to root through his closet. Freddy's dad was a bartender at the Rivertowne Inn, and had worked there for as long as anyone could remember.

"He's okay . . . you know, he's Dad," Freddy said, shrugging.

"He's still at the Rivertowne, right? They couldn't run that place without him."

"Yeah, he's still there," Freddy acknowledged, a bit discouraged "They switched him to the overnight shift. They've got him doing prep work now, placing orders, checking inventory. He's been bartending there for most of my life, and now—"

"They demoted him?" Dennis stopped packing, and was more engaged in the conversation.

"Sort of, yeah. I don't know why. He always works hard, he's always on time, but he's slowing up a little bit. It's not that he's too old for the job. I think he's just . . . tired. I wish he would have done something more with his life. He could have gone to school, and done a lot more than he has. He's absolutely brilliant with numbers."

"Ah, don't be too hard on the old man," Dennis replied. Freddy's dad, Fred Sr., was always a bit of a sore spot with Freddy. Freddy loved his dad, but there was always tension in their relationship. Freddy was an overachiever, who proudly touted his Mongolian heritage. Fred Sr. was content with his job and just being part of the community. "Your dad is a good man, and he always did what was best for you."

"You're right. He's just so smart, and I feel like he's wasting his life there."

"Maybe the changes at work will motivate him to try something different."

Freddy nodded in hopeful agreement, as Dennis finished packing

CHAPTER 2

"Do you remember that day in high school when we met?" Freddy asked, smiling.

Dennis sipped from his beer and smirked, as he and Freddy lounged on his back porch after he'd finished packing.

"Freshman year, gym class," Freddy began, even though Dennis knew it all.

Dennis met Mark and Freddy at Verona High School although their families had known each other and gone to school together forever. Generations of families had lived and died, together, in Verona. That's the way it had always been, the way it would always be. But the boys didn't become friendly until their freshman year of high school. The life-changing event happened during gym class. The class was playing dodge ball. Mark and Freddy had both been hit, and were out of the game, which was fine by them. Even in their freshman year, Mark and Freddy were different than the rest of the kids. They were more interested in Dungeons & Dragons than Verona High Tide football.

With the sound of bouncing volleyballs careening off the gym's wooden floors and cement walls, Mark and Freddy were standing on the sidelines, waiting for the game to be over. A few senior football players decided that they'd rather throw balls at the underclassmen on the sidelines, than throw balls with the kids who were still in play.

After dodging and ducking, and getting hit a few times, Mark leaped to the top of the ancient metal bleachers, raised both arms, as if he were about to part the Red Sea, and shouted, "By the power of Vollrath, I command your arms to become heavy, as if filled with sand!"

The next ball was thrown with such velocity that other students in the gym claimed that they heard it hiss. It hit Mark squarely on the bridge of his nose, launching him from the bleachers, to the hard wooden floor below. He was a pimply-faced, freshman mess, as blood gushed from his sundial nose.

"That one's for Vollrath," the seniors howled, "whoever that is!"

Dennis boldly walked toward the seniors, as they cocked their rippled arms to fire a ball at Freddy. Everyone knew Dennis was The Brad's brother.

"Not too smart, guys," Dennis coolly said to them. "I heard there'll be some college scouts at the game this Friday. If you'd like to have some passes thrown your way, I suggest you stop."

Dennis stood his ground, staring down the seniors. The seniors stared back for a moment, and then turned, angrily slamming their volleyballs to the ground. Lumbering away, they grumbled to themselves.

Dennis watched them walk away, and then headed over to check on Mark. By that time, Mr. Chieffo, the gym teacher, was holding an ice pack on Mark's nose.

"Danks, Dens. Di dreally dappreciate dat," Mark said.

"He said he really appreciates that," Freddy interpreted. "Me too."

"Yeah, no problem," Dennis replied, calmly. "By the way," he added, "who's Vollrath?"

"He'd da dreat dor—" Mark began, but Freddy cut him off with a hand.

"I got it. We can't understand what you're saying, anyway. Vollrath is a powerful sorcerer in our LARP faction. Sometimes Mark freaks out and thinks that, just because something works on a LARP battlefield, it will work in the real world."

"It dwill domeday," Mark said.

"Oh . . . What's a LARP?"

"LARP stands for Live Action Role Play." Freddy spit out the words in a hurry, trying to get them out before Dennis walked away. Since he was The Brad's brother, Dennis probably had an appointment to cut class with a cheerleader. "There's a group of us that get together, dress up like medieval characters, and stage battles in the Outlook Woods here in Verona. It's pretty cool."

[19]

"Um, yeah," Dennis said, still a bit puzzled, and thinking that the whole thing sounded like a colossal waste of time.

The swelling inside Mark's nose had gone down a bit, and he was able to speak.

Mark readjusted his glasses, his bony fingers still holding the icepack. "And we're a Live Combat group, not a wuss Theater Style group. Our group brings it every weekend in the woods to whoever wants some!" Mark said, as if daring Dennis to say or think otherwise.

"And you use real swords?" Dennis asked.

"No, they're high-quality Finnish fiberglass wrapped in imported Dutch foam. Finnish fiberglass is much better than the fiberglass that the Danes put out. And the Dutch, well, they've mastered the art of foam creation, but the Canadians are quickly approaching the Dutch in terms of quality and development," Mark replied, sounding like an international fiberglass and foam expert. He paused, expecting Dennis to contribute to the fiberglass/foam conversation.

"So . . . you 'bring it' with fiberglass swords?" Dennis countered, trying not to laugh.

"Yeah, we bring it with fiberglass swords," Freddy said, defensively, sensing the usual pattern of ridicule. "There are kill rules, and a narrative that we follow. I'm among the bloodline of a great and fierce line of proud Mongolian warriors, and our LARP group is as realistic as it gets. Why don't you join us this Saturday at Outlook . . . or doesn't The Brad's brother mix with people like us?" Although Freddy was small and wiry, he gave off an intensity that Dennis normally didn't see among the non-jock set. His high cheekbones gave his face an added air of stoic strength.

It was a bold move on Dennis's part, to indirectly use The Brad's name to defend two freshman geeks. Hanging out with Mark and Freddy in public wouldn't exactly help him win Homecoming King, either.

Dennis's social status was like a light switch. Prior to that day in gym class, it was permanently ON. He was The Brad's brother, after all. After that day, it was permanently OFF. He was friends with them, after all. Once the switch was OFF, Dennis was The Brad's little brother only by blood, not in social status. And in high school, especially in a small place like Verona, social status is everything.

"Yeah, I've thought a lot about that day," Dennis said, finishing the rest of his beer. "I have no idea why I did that. I wonder if things would have been different if I had just let those goons pummel you two." He said the last part with a teasing smile.

"FYI, the pummeling was about to end, because I was about to administer some Mongolian justice on those two clowns." Freddy believed that the military history of his Mongolian heritage gave him an edge in every battle, be it LARP, chess or dodge ball.

"Good thing that didn't happen," Dennis wisecracked.

"Yeah, well, I'll show you what I mean this weekend," Freddy declared, determined.

Dennis hadn't known anything about the LARP lifestyle until he met Mark and Freddy. He got into it because they became friends, and he wanted to share a common interest. Slowly, his interest grew, and he looked forward to the annual trek to Uniontown every year for the KNEL (Knights, Nobles, and Elegant Ladies) convention. KNEL was a LARPer's dream, with vendors who sold realistic battle gear, authentic food, home-brewed beer and mead. It also had a LARP tournament that almost guaranteed national recognition to the winner— within the LARP community, of course. Dennis, Freddy and Mark hoped to place highly in the tournament this year. Uniontown was 115 miles away, but it was well worth the trip.

Dennis took a last swig, got up and put the empty bottles in the recycling bin.

"Would you mind picking up Mark and driving him to Uniontown? I just don't feel like dealing with his Markness the whole way there," Dennis asked, as they walked to Freddy's car. Mark didn't drive, so either Dennis or Freddy had to take him to their LARP activities.

"Yeah, sure, no problem," Freddy replied. He was willing to

make any accommodations necessary to ensure Dennis's full participation this weekend.

"Cool. Okay, well . . . see you in Uniontown," Dennis said, as Freddy got into his car. Freddy smiled and nodded, turning the ignition. Driving to Mark's house, seeing Dennis in the rear view mirror, Freddy had a sick feeling in his stomach.

*   *   *

Mark lived in his parents' attic, and was a professional Internet auction buyer/seller. He had his own Internet auction site, Magical Mark's Toy Kingdom, which bought and sold collectible toys and had a separate LARP section to buy and sell LARP gear. You could find Mark at the toy store in Verona, and even on the mainland, buying up the latest toys. He'd take them home, pack them up in specially sealed, airtight plastic bins and let them sit for years—to enhance their value. Mark was certain that his toys, and the proper storage thereof, would make him a very rich man in his old age.

Like most things in Mark's life, packing toys was a very involved, complicated process. It was almost like he was making wine. Mark had a list of steps that he'd developed, which he followed to the letter. He would pack the toys in a light-restricted room, to prevent further sun damage. Mark never touched the toys when packing, because he didn't want the acid from his fingers to damage packaging. Instead, he would use rubber-tipped tongs, the kind used to pick ice out of a bowl, to handle his treasures. He would carefully roll the toys in cellophane using the tongs, followed by aluminum foil to block out any light, and a final layer of bubble wrap to protect them from accidental impact. Mark had set up an area of his large, loft-style room that he used for storage. He had several gun safes in the storage part of his room, and was careful to buy safes that had metal shelves, not plastic, because plastic shelves would melt if the house caught on fire. Each safe was connected to a furnace/AC unit that was separate from the main unit that controlled the temperature in the house. The safes, or "vaults" as

Mark called them, were always set to 67.8 degrees, and had a generator backup in the event of a power failure. He'd let the toys sit and age properly, and then sell them online within a few years.

Mark was fiercely devoted to LARP, and would often become unreasonable if anything got in the way of creating an authentic LARP experience during a competition. Maps of all the battlefields, which the group would be visiting throughout the year, covered the walls of his bedroom. Each map was similar, yet different, in that they were all of the same area. However, they detailed different LARP storylines, and battles that had been fought, or would be fought.

He was also the local GM, or Game Master, for all LARP activities that took place in Outlook Woods, a huge forested area in Verona. It was Mark's job to come up with the details and storylines of the LARP activities to be played out in the woods. He was known, even in the mainland, as a master LARP storyteller and organizer. He was also a total Immersionist. When Mark went into battle, he was Vollrath.

Freddy, on the other hand, loved LARP from the aspect that it allowed him to get in touch with his "inner warrior". Freddy's family was originally from Mongolia, and arrived in the United States around eighty years before. Freddy was very much into his heritage and culture, and was incredibly close with his family. During LARP combat, Freddy was often misjudged because of his small stature, but his size was his greatest strength because it pushed him to defy expectations. Freddy never wanted to let his friends or family down, and those in his inner circle knew that they could count on him.

Freddy claimed that his family was a family of great Mongolian warriors, dating back to the third century. As a financial consultant for the Kiss beverage company located in Verona, Freddy always said that he felt "neutered" by life. Inside, he was a brave Mongolian warrior. Outside, he was a suit, running for his cheese in the rat race. So LARP gave Freddy an opportunity to do battle as his ancestors had done in a relatively safe environment.

Freddy arrived at Mark's house to take him to Uniontown. Mark's front door was always open, so Freddy walked right in and headed up to Mark's room on the top floor.

"You ready?" Freddy asked, as he walked up the steps.

"Shhhhh."

"What?"

"Shhhhh. I got you now, baby."

Freddy moved cautiously up the steps. With Mark, you never knew what you'd find.

"Come to me, Captain Luke, come to me." Mark was chanting over and over, mantra-like. "Ha! Gotcha! Mine, mine, mine!!!"

Freddy suspiciously stopped in the doorway, a few feet behind Mark. Mark was sitting at his computer, the blue glow of the monitor filling an otherwise, dark, wood-paneled room.

Mark turned to Freddy, as if this was a normal scene in everyone's life. "Hey, what's up?"

"You tell me."

"Well," Mark began, his arms flailing. "I was just on an online auction and I won an original Trek Wars Captain Luke action figure from 1978. Original packaging and everything! Do you know what this means?"

"It means you'll have another toy to play with in the tub?"

"No!" Mark said, ignoring Freddy's comment. "It means that I now own one of the rarest action figures ever. It means that it will be here in a few days. It means that I will store it in an airtight, lightproof container, and sell it for a boatload of cash in about five years. I could only get a truckload of cash for it now. I'm holding out for a boatload." He smiled, waiting to be praised for his victory.

"Must be a small boat," Freddy answered.

Mark sighed in disgust at Freddy's lack of appreciation. "Whatever. Point is, I just sniped some guy in Texas for it. Who says Texans are the best shots?"

"Are you ready to go to Uniontown?" said Freddy, bored.

"Yeah, but I'm worried about him. I think we're gonna lose him," Mark replied, his mood souring.

"You're always worried we're gonna lose him. He's not going anywhere," Freddy answered dismissively.

"No, really, I think we're coming to a point where he's gonna quit on us,"

"Why?"

"Well, I talked to him yesterday, and he really didn't have a battle plan set for Uniontown. He didn't seem to care, either. This is a big deal, Freddy." Mark's voice was getting louder and more excited. "And he's Sir Den-flippin'-gar. He's got a reputation to uphold! He's gotta help represent V Town!! We gotta whup those mainland wusses!!! He can't just run around the woods of Uniontown aimlessly, can he? Can he?" Mark, frustrated and out of breath, reached for his inhaler.

"Of course not," Freddy said, calmly. He was trying to get Mark to calm down, if for no other reason than he didn't want to to give him CPR.

"Look," Mark said, careful to control his breathing, "I don't think that Dennis has his heart in it anymore. I think he's just doing it because he's done it forever and is worried that it will affect our friendship in some way if he quits. I'm afraid we're losing him to the real world, where good versus evil just doesn't matter anymore."

"Well, look, I'll talk to him and try to feel him out. If I think he's gonna quit, I'll hear him out and try to change his mind. It's all we can do, really. If he quits, we'll still be friends, I'm sure," Freddy reassured. He knew how much their friendship meant to Mark, and how LARP was sort of a reminder to Mark of when they were all younger. Mark was always looking backward, and, lately, Dennis was always looking forward, with Freddy stuck in the middle.

There was silence, as the idea of Dennis quitting marinated in their minds. If Dennis quit, did it mean that they should quit, too? Were they getting too old for LARP? Maybe they should investigate the "real world" a little bit more.

Freddy finally spoke. "Does Jen know her role for this weekend?"

"Oh, crap!" Mark jumped up, and rummaged through the

mess of his room, trying to find his phone. "I forgot to call her to check!"

He found the phone under a pile of fake chain-mail. He dialed, the phone rang, and a female voice answered.

"Hey, you sexy sea elf. What's good, baby?" Mark purred, seductively.

"Yeah, I know what to do. See you at the hotel."

Mark paused, expecting more. But the only response he heard was the dial tone.

"Everything cool?" Freddy asked.

"Oh, yeah," Mark said, trying to recover. "She said she'll meet us at the hotel and that she can't wait to see me."

"Too bad you can't create a LARP in which Jen actually knows you exist. That would be a big score for you! Sexy sea elf? Are you kidding me?"

Mark became defensive. "Yeah, sexy sea elf. That was her character last year at Uniontown. You gotta admit that she looked amazing in her blue body paint, right? C'mon, I know you still think about it."

Freddy headed down the steps without saying a word. Mark grabbed his luggage and followed him. "Like I'm the only one who thinks a woman painted blue is hot," he said to himself.

Since Freddy had to take a detour to pick up Mark, Dennis had a bit of a lead in driving to Uniontown. As he drove to the Hulton Bridge, which was the only bridge that connected Verona to the mainland, he looked at the amazing scenery of the tiny island.

Verona was an island town located two miles off the coast of the state of Washington. The Pacific Ocean flowed to Verona, through the Strait of Juan de Fuca. With a population a little under three thousand, Verona was big enough to have its own school district, but small enough that everyone knew everyone else. The phrase "you go there once, you'll be there twice" perfectly described Verona. The island was self-sufficient, with its own grocery store, hardware store, two strip malls, a movie theater, and a bank; the residents enjoyed their independence.

Verona was a very blue collar island, mostly filled with mills and production plants, including the world headquarters for the famed "Kiss" drink, a sugary fruit-flavored drink that was packaged in a hand-sized bottle that looked like a set of lips. Kiss drinks were sold all over the world, but were a staple of the diet for kids on the island. The huge Kiss plant employed hundreds of Veronaites.

Veronaites were not as economically successful as the people on the mainland, but they were just as happy. Verona was a picturesque island, surrounded by water, and enriched by beautiful foliage. Veronaites were very outdoorsy. Families would spend weekends hunting and hiking in the beautiful woodlands that could be found in and around nearly every neighborhood. The Verona woods were interconnected and went on for miles. It wasn't uncommon for a Verona family to get a year's worth of meat from a winter's hunting expedition.

Socially, Verona stopped paying attention to the rest of the world sometime after 1960. While the citizens had all the modern conveniences, the atmosphere of the island was very folksy. Neighbors still took walks at night, stopped to visit one another, and showed genuine concern and compassion for those around them. No matter where you went in Verona, you'd always run into someone, somewhere, who knew someone in your family.

Everyone attended the annual Verona Fair in June, rode the Ferris wheel, ate the famous Rivertowne grilled fish sandwiches, and went home happy. At the Fall Festival, there was the apple cider competition and leaf-raking event. Wintertime brought the Festival of Lights, when every tree and bush in Riverview Park was adorned with multicolored bulbs, and local church choirs caroled while the citizens "awwwed" at the display. In the spring was the competition for the best garden on the island.

Verona was a different place, tucked into a different time.

Dennis slowed down as he approached the Hulton Bridge. In Verona, a traffic jam was ten or more cars trying to get to the same place at the same time. The Hulton Bridge was an old, lilac-colored, single-lane bridge, so it didn't take much to back it up. Before the Hulton Bridge existed, a ferry, operated by

Jonathan Hulton, was the only way to get to and from the mainland.

Dennis sent Freddy a text: *Bridge backed up. Take ur time.*

Thnx, Freddy texted back. *M worried u will quit this wkend.*

He should b, Dennis typed.

It had been almost ten years since Dennis had met Mark and Freddy. After the initial awkwardness of "The Brad's" brother joining the unpopular crowd, Dennis, Mark and Freddy enjoyed a smooth friendship. Although Dennis gave Mark a hard time—everyone gave Mark a hard time—he really did care about him.

There were many, many times over the last ten years when Dennis was there for Mark, and vice versa. Dennis saved Mark on the LARP battlefield more times than he could remember. With LARP, Mark's reach always exceeded his grasp. If he were capable of taking on two opponents, he would always challenge the entire team, just to prove himself—and he always did prove himself, just not in the way he anticipated.

Even though Mark dropped out of college, he spent lots of time helping Dennis with class projects. Dennis always felt that he owed Mark at least half of his diploma.

When Mark's grandfather died while they were in high school, Dennis served as a pall bearer with Mark and the rest of Mark's cousins. Dennis could still see Mark's grandma's face, tears streaming down her chapped cheeks, saying to him, "You're like a grandson to me."

LARP was the third person in their relationship. It was their common bond, but it was also driving Dennis away from Mark. Their time together outside of LARP activities was always fun, but Mark's need to control everything LARP-related had slowly driven a wedge between the two friends. It's not that Dennis wanted to control their LARP events, it's that Mark's inability to reason made it more of a job for Dennis, instead of a hobby.

It wasn't all bad memories, though. Dennis had a lot of good times at Uniontown, and in the Outlook Woods. Mark was Vollrath the sorcerer during their LARP battles, and it always amazed Dennis at how easily the other LARPers would fall under any "spell" that Mark cast upon them. Mark turned a whole army into frogs once, and the people actually played along! They dropped their weapons, got down on all fours, and hopped away. Dennis smiled at the memory of seeing thirty people, adults no less, acting like frogs. But what comes around goes around. Mark was once put under a spell that forced him to take his clothes off, down to his superhero underwear, and climb a tree. It took him a few tries to get up there, and by the time he did climb it, he was covered in scratches from the bark. The best part, for his opponents, was that he had to stay in the tree until dusk. Because he was a dedicated LARPer, Mark went along with it, much to the humor of the rest of his army.

Dennis had played the freshman gym class episode over and over again in his head for the last ten years. What if he had let the seniors throw balls at Mark and Freddy? What would have been the harm? How did two kids getting hit in the head directly affect him? If Dennis hadn't stopped that assault, would he have been the social successor to "The Brad"? Would he have been the next big Verona football star, complete with head cheerleader arm candy? Why did he stand up for two kids he barely knew?

Maybe he did it because he intrinsically knew that he didn't want to be "The Dennis". Look at Brad. He was still "The Brad", even though he was approaching thirty. Brad's existence, even in high school, was pretty shallow. Some people peak in high school; they'll never be any smarter, better looking, or popular, than they were at seventeen. The Friday football games, the Friday night after-party, getting wasted all weekend, slapping cheerleaders on the butt as you pass them in the hall (Brad always did it with a backhand, calling it 'The Bradhand', like it was an award), finding a nerd to do your homework so that you could go to a top college for free on a football scholarship. All of that had a shelf life.

Besides, Dennis hated football. That was Brad's thing, and look what it got him; two bad knees, years of bitterness, and a bunch of trite high school stories.

Dennis didn't have any of the typical college stories to tell. He attended Seattle State College with Mark and Freddy, and the three of them spent most of their free time writing new LARP scenarios, and storylines, for the summer. Dennis never got drunk and woke up next to a girl whose name he had forgotten. He never streaked through the hallowed halls of Seattle State College. He never went to a single frat party.

But there was always the thought in the back of his mind that he was missing something by devoting so much time to his hobby. He had a longing for something different, and he didn't know what it was, or if all the time he spent LARPing over the years had caused it.

No, Dennis didn't want to be Brad forever. But, it would have been cool to be Brad for a week during his senior year at Verona High. Just to see what it was like. The respect. The promise. The potential. The girls. Just for a week.

At the age of twenty-three, most of the dates he'd had were with LARP girls (What was it like to date a girl who had no idea what the difference was between a sorcerer and a mage?), and he hadn't dated a non-LARPer since the few dates he had had with Alyssa in high school.

Alyssa was beautiful, both inside and out. She was the type of person that people were drawn to, not because of her appearance, although she might have been one of the best looking girls at Verona High, but because of her presence. Call it charisma, energy, whatever it was—Alyssa had it.

When Alyssa smiled, she smiled with her entire being.

She could have been a cheerleader, head cheerleader, in fact, but she hadn't gone that route because she wasn't a follower. Alyssa wouldn't be caught dead cheering for a team because she was "supposed" to; she did everything because she wanted to. She didn't care about social status, what was "in", or who was "out"—Alyssa was ruled by her heart. .

CHAPTER 3

Dennis arrived at Eiler's Hotel in Uniontown, and was unpacking his SUV, as Freddy and Mark pulled in next to him. Mark began questioning Dennis before both feet had even hit the ground.

"What's the hotel business? I thought we were Yurting it?"

"Nice to see you, too." Dennis smiled.

"Really, every year at Uniontown we build an awesome Yurt and we stay in the woods. It helps us get into character. I feel the forest that way," Mark said, dramatically. "I don't know if I can bring my 'A' game if I'm in some hotel with electricity and running water. I want to sleep in the Yurt."

"Sorry, I'm not Yurting anything. I'm staying in the hotel, with TV, air conditioning, running water, and a toilet that doesn't smell like a Rosedale ogre's butt. And honestly, if I'm spending a few hours driving to Uniontown, I'd at least like to get a good night's sleep," Dennis countered.

"Oh, how the mighty have fallen," Mark said, his head in his hand. "How can we be great medieval warriors this weekend if we're using twenty-first century accommodations?"

"We'll manage," Dennis replied, then added, "Plus, Jen will be staying here, too. Maybe you'll catch a glimpse of her doing yoga in the hotel gym."

The image silenced Mark, as he considered the possibility.

Jen was Dennis's friend. She worked at the Seattle Museum as curator in the medieval hall where Dennis, Freddy, and Mark spent time researching battle armor and medieval battle history. She was introduced to LARP by the group, and their relationship was strictly platonic. Except for Mark, who seemed to think that Jen was romantically interested in him, regardless of how many times she said that she wasn't.

Off the battlefield, her shoulder-length chestnut hair, and hipster glasses, projected the image of academia she needed for her job. At work, Jen was a quiet, unassuming, bookish type, but her sharp wit and quick smile hinted at her true character. There were countless times when Dennis would see an opposing army smile victoriously when they saw Jen coming. Jen saw the smiles, too, and loved it. Dennis often thought that Jen played up the "defenseless maiden" angle on the battlefield because she so thoroughly enjoyed running her dagger through the chest of her surprised opponent. "Betcha didn't see that coming, huh?" Jen would say with a smile and sexy wink, as she left yet another opponent "dead" on the field. Jen's skill, and toned, athletic body had won more battles than Dennis could remember.

Just then, Mark's cell phone rang. He checked the caller ID and said, "Business call, gotta take it," and he walked off to the end of the parking lot, where Freddy and Dennis heard Mark shout, "what do you mean it's not an authentic 1978 Captain Luke???"

Freddy and Dennis heard footsteps behind them, and turned to see Jen. "Okay, so who told him I was coming?" she accused, hands on her hips.

Freddy and Dennis just looked at each other, not wanting to answer.

"Um . . . yeah, okay it was me," Dennis replied, meekly raising his hand. "I really didn't tell him, it just kinda came out."

Jen shook her head in mock disgust "You know, when a girl wants to get her LARP on, she doesn't want to be followed around by someone murmuring love spells under his breath."

"Well, hopefully things will change after this weekend," Dennis said.

"What's that supposed to mean?" Jen replied, confused. "Are we gonna pay some LARP queen to keep Mark busy during league play?"

Dennis pondered the idea for a minute, but then got back on track. "No, I think I'm going to take some time off for a while. From LARPing."

Jen walked toward Dennis, her index finger waving. "Oh no, there's no way I'm doing this without you. I couldn't tolerate a weekend trip without you keeping him in check."

[32]

"Great," Freddy said, throwing his hand up "There goes half of our planning team."

"Jen, c'mon," Dennis said "You can't just quit because I'm taking time off."

"No, *you* c'mon," Jen replied as she looked Dennis squarely in his light blue eyes "I've been watching you over the last few months. You're not thinking of taking time off, you're thinking of quitting."

Dennis looked away. He could see Mark, still on the phone, manically jumping up and down.

Dennis looked again at Jen. "I don't know what I'm going to do. I just know that if I don't quit, or take some time off, our collective friendship is really going to suffer. And LARP isn't worth losing any of you. Not even Mark."

Jen looked at Freddy, who helplessly shrugged.

"If anyone has the right to leave here, it's me," Jen continued. "I gotta put up with Mark sending me texts, asking how the Law of Justinian influenced the building of Destrier. And I've mentally blocked out the other texts and emails he sends me."

Freddy and Dennis elbowed each other, trying to stifle their laughter. They'd witnessed Mark's "game" over the years, and it was always horrible. Poor Jen. It was a good thing she could handle herself.

"But, see, that's the point of this," said Jen, who was now laughing with Dennis and Freddy. She was firmly in on the joke that was her "relationship" with Mark. "We've got some really great stories to tell. When we're old and sitting around a campfire together, we can reminisce about all the great times we had."

"Yeah, but who wants to hear about the time I fell in a creek while battling on a log, got soaking wet, and my cheap breeches ripped, exposing my family jewels to the opposing army?" Dennis countered.

Freddy and Jen smiled and snickered at the memory, but quickly composed themselves when they realized that Dennis was serious.

"Well, look, this weekend means a lot to Mark, so please give it your all just this one last time. After that, we'll talk about the future, okay?" Freddy begged.

Dennis exhaled deeply. "Okay . . . fine."

"Good. I'll see you guys later. I need to get out of here before Mark spots me," Jen said as she glanced over her shoulder.

A few minutes later, Mark returned to the fold. He was talking through his gritted teeth, his thin lips almost sneering. "Lying Internet cretins! That was the guy I bought the Captain Luke from. It's not from '78, it's from '98! It's not an original Trek Wars figure; it's from those crappy sequels! He said it was a typo, and that he was sorry. Sorry doesn't do me any good, I can't resell sorry." The gang stared blankly at Mark. They'd seen this before. All they could do was let him express his frustration, get it out of his system, and move on. Mark was oblivious to their stares, as he focused intensely on his hands "I'd like to put a spell on him that would turn all ten of his fingers into 1978 model Captain Luke action figures, so that he'd know exactly what they looked like. And then you know what I'd do . . . I'd cut off each Captain Luke finger and sell them. That would be a lesson he'd never forget."

Mark slowly raised his head, and stared at his friends. There was silence. When Mark realized his inner monolog had escaped, again, and that his friends weren't nodding in agreement, he quickly recovered. "So . . . anyone need help unpacking?" .

CHAPTER 4

It was shortly after dusk when everyone made it to their rooms to decompress. The parking lot was packed with every car imaginable, from beat-up Toyotas, to sturdy family mini-vans, to pristine Cadillacs. But what they all had in common was a LARP bumper sticker. It wasn't unusual to see "I break for Warlocks" or "Real men carry wands" on their bumpers. The LARP participants who attended the convention were vast and varied. There were people like Mark, who still lived with their parents and collected toys, but there were also a fair share of highly paid professionals raising armies to participate in this yearly tradition.

Dennis was out of town on business a few years ago, and needed an emergency root canal. He went to a dentist the hotel recommended, and realized that the dentist was someone he'd slain on the battlefield a month before. Root canals are scary enough without having a guy you just pummeled working on you. Dennis and Freddy often talked about how funny it was to see people working their boring 9-to-5 jobs, all dressed up in their suits, trying to act like adults, and then see them the following weekend dressed like some fantasy character wielding a crossbow.

The hotel was unusually crowded, which was another indication to Dennis that his LARPing days were coming to a close. In the old days, all the LARPers would sleep in Yurts on the battlefield. Now, in their 'old' age, they were staying in a hotel. A three-star hotel, no less. Now that everyone was older and could afford it, they chose convenience over authenticity. More proof for Dennis that maybe this time in his life had passed.

Uniontown wasn't a place that anyone visited, or went to for a vacation, or really even thought about. In fact, the town was made up of a few strip malls, a couple of hotels, and lots of open fields and forests. In some ways, it was sort of like a bigger version of Verona, except it was on the mainland. The annual KNEL festival was something of a holiday for the people of Uniontown, because it boosted their economy and flooded the town with tourists. After KNEL, Uniontown went back to being just another anonymous, sleepy, Washington town.

The KNEL convention was one of the largest of its kind, certainly the biggest on the West Coast. The convention also offered LARP history classes, workshops in different ancient forms of combat, and mobile stores that sold everything LARP related; battle gear, T-shirts, period cookbooks and combat training DVDs. Some of the local Uniontown restaurants got into the spirit every year, and transformed themselves into medieval period restaurants, where pigs were cooked on spits in the parking lot, and the occasional (staged) swordfight would take place during dinner.

Later that evening at the hotel, the group was sitting in the lobby, watching TV. Mark was still moaning about not staying in a Yurt, but his attitude quickly changed when he saw Jen.

"Hey, luscious," Mark said slyly, springing up to greet her.

"Thanks and no," Jen automatically replied, sailing past him, toward the front desk.

Freddy and Dennis grinned at each other. Mark trying to hook up with Jen was as old as the battle between good and evil. It made the group friendship awkward at first, but now everyone was used to it. And Mark never let Jen's attitude stop him from trying.

"She's cracking," Mark said, with quiet determination. "We will consummate our love this weekend. First, victory on the battlefield. Then, victory with my maiden. It is decidedly so."

"Well, until that miraculous event occurs, there's only two things to do in Uniontown; LARP and drink," Freddy proclaimed.

Like a well-rehearsed comedy routine, Jen appeared. "And I don't see no trolls!"

"But I do see a bar!" said Dennis. He was starting to relax and get with the festive mood of the weekend. Maybe this wouldn't be so bad after all.

"Let's get hammered!" Freddy exclaimed, as he put his arms around Jen and Dennis. They merrily headed to the hotel bar.

"No, no, NO!" Mark scolded, like an uptight parent.

The three stopped in their tracks. They knew what was coming.

"We don't drink the night before a battle."

Dennis, Freddy and Jen turned around and looked at Mark blankly.

"The last thing I need tomorrow is a bunch of hung-over warriors. Not only is it totally unprofessional, but it's also a health hazard. What if one of you has a spear coming at you, and you're too hung over to move in time. Then what? I'll tell you . . . you'll be dead. We can't have that tomorrow. No drinking."

"If I'm hung over, I won't feel it as much. To the bar!!!" Freddy shot back.

The three marched into the bar, with Mark trailing behind, shaking his head disapprovingly.

The bar was filled with LARPers, some already in costume. There was a karaoke contest going on, with the LARPers singing each song using an olde English accent, which fit perfectly with their character and costume. Other LARPers chose to sing in the created language that went along with their character.

In the last several years, as his interest in the actual battle waned, Dennis enjoyed the nights at the bar more than the battles. It wasn't the alcohol he enjoyed, it was the LARPers themselves. All of these people came from all over the country, some from around the world, to this undistinguished place called Uniontown, just for this festival. Every day, these people had to live by society's rules. They had to act a certain way, dress a certain way, and, oftentimes, couldn't talk freely about their hobby because most people either didn't understand it, or thought it was ridiculous. But, during this one weekend a year, they were the normal ones, and everyone else was an outcast. They could be who they were, talk about what was important to them, be it warlocks, sci-fi, or the latest advancements in LARP hybrid body armor.

"This weekend will be great," Dennis said to himself. "It will be okay."

Around midnight, one of the LARPers, usually someone who played a king or duke, would get roaring drunk and their character would take over. Tonight was no exception.

"Attention everyone, attention please," a slightly-built man said over the karaoke microphone. "His Royal Highness, the mighty, wise, and beloved, King Peacock, has an announcement to make." The slightly-built man bowed respectfully, handed the microphone to a larger man, and backed away.

"Greetings my loyal subjects," bellowed King Peacock in a faux proper British accent, circa tenth century.

"Greetings, your grace," the crowd responded, playing along.

"It has come to my royal attention that many of you here enjoy the consumption of ale. Is this true?"

The crowd applauded and cheered.

The King continued. "It is my prerogative, then, to supply you with all of the ale that you are able to consume. Leave no bottle filled, leave no tap undisturbed! Drink hearty, all of you, for tonight King Peacock will pay your tab!!!"

The crowd erupted in shouts of delight and high-fives.

"Good thing Peacock just got promoted to principal of his school," Dennis said to Jen, as they headed for the bar. "Tonight's gonna cost him!" Even Mark made his way to the bar, saying, "Who am I to turn down a direct order from a king?" .

CHAPTER 5

The next day everyone met for breakfast at the hotel's restaurant. Mark showed up late, looking bad, and feeling worse.

"Hey, luscious," Jen purred to Mark as he sat down. She was teasing, of course, but it didn't matter. Mark was too hung over to respond, even if her come-on had been sincere. "Aww, baby, c'mon," Jen continued to Mark. "You gotta pull it together. You have a big battle today and I want you to be my big strong man out there. I love a man who can party all night and slay all day."

Mark brightened, though dimly. "Really?"

Jen became serious again. "Depends on the man. Honestly, I just want you to sober up so you don't yak on me during battle. Can you manage that for me?"

Mark grunted as the waitress poured him a cup of coffee.

"So," Dennis said to Jen, changing subjects, "are you gonna go see your dad at Fort Lewis?"

"Yeah, if he has time. He's overseeing some drills today. A general's work is never done, I guess." Jen's dad was a general in the US Army and stationed at Fort Lewis, Washington. The general embraced Jen's love of LARP. He saw it as a safer alternative to the family tradition of military service.

Many LARPers were in the restaurant having their breakfast. Some of them were dressed for battle, and some of them were still in their pajamas. Joe Peacock, AKA King Peacock, sat at the table near Dennis, Freddy, Mark, and Jen.

"Good morning, your grace," Freddy shouted over to Joe.

"Not so loud, please," Joe responded, quietly. Joe always spoke quietly, even on the battlefield, but this quiet was more of a necessity, than a practice.

"How are you feeling?" Dennis asked Joe.

"I have a ferocious headache, and am $1,200 lighter. That's how I'm feeling." Joe's hair was always perfectly groomed, and he was always properly attired for the day. The morning after he paid for a night of revelry, his hair was a coppery mess, and he was wearing sweatpants, slippers, and a T-shirt that read Property of Northgate High.

"Well, if it's any consolation," Jen interjected, with a smile, "all the bottles were emptied, and no taps were undisturbed. We followed orders, your highness."

"Great . . ." Joe said, with a heavy, exhausted sigh.

Changing topics, Freddy asked Joe, "So, you're our king this weekend, right?"

Before Joe could answer, Mark came out of his haze and spoke, irritated at Freddy for not knowing who was who this weekend. "Yes, Freddy, Joe is the King. We will be defending him this weekend. How many times did we go over this in the car on the way over? And how many times did we go over this at home, before we even left? I wrote it all out over the last year, the back story behind our Kingdom and everything. This weekend, Joe is The King, and we're battling the LARP group from Oakmont, remember?"

Freddy was both incensed and embarrassed at Mark's admonishment. Dennis squirmed in his seat. It was already happening.

Jen looked at Mark, in disgust. "So he forgot, what's the big deal? It was a long night last night. And if it wasn't for Freddy, you would have had to ride a bus to get here. And we know how well you'd do there. So I'd back off if I were you."

Just then, members of the Oakmont LARP faction walked into the restaurant. They were fully clothed, in character, and ready for battle.

"See, that's what I'm talking about," Mark said, ignoring Jen, and nodding in the direction of the Oakmont crew. "Look at those guys. It's 9:30 in the morning, the battle doesn't start for another few hours, and they're dressed and ready to go. That's dedication. They probably got their attacks and formations memorized and everything. They look like they could come over here and slay us at any minute."

"Right after they have the Mr. Waffle Special and Strawberry Slim Smoothie, of course," Jen said, sarcastically.

"I just hope we're ready for what's gonna happen today," Mark replied under his breath.

"Check please," Dennis said to a passing waitress. As soon as he started to have a good time, Mark always ruined it with his obnoxious intensity. Mark didn't see these trips as chances to get away with friends and have a good time. It always came back to winning the war game.

As the group headed back to their rooms to put on their costumes, Mark made yet another stop at the bathroom. His stomach wasn't used to a night of merriment. As they waited for Mark, Dennis spoke aloud to himself, and to Jen and Freddy.

"This is why I'm pretty much done coming to these events. Almost every year, I hate coming, but I get here and I have a good time. Then he ruins it by acting like a brat. We're not playing for money, and if we win, we get a dumb little plastic trophy. I'm just here to have fun. Period. With him it's like work."

Freddy, worried that Dennis was going to walk off and not return, tried to calm him down.

"I know. We're all uncomfortable with it. All we can do is get through this weekend and straighten it out when we get back to Verona."

Dennis glared at Jen and Freddy. "One more outburst from him, and I'm gone. We're not in our teens anymore, and I really have no interest in dealing with it. I'm only here for you guys, 'cause I promised I'd come. I'm not gonna flake out like other LARPers do. But I'm only going to deal with so much. I've got better things to do than to run around a field with him shouting orders at me."

Mark exited the bathroom, looking paler than when he entered. There was an uncomfortable minute, and then everyone headed to their rooms in silence.

Dennis was Sir Den-gar, a heroic and proud warrior. He feared nothing, took on anything, and was the physical anchor of the team. He wasn't a large man, maybe six feet tall and 180lbs, but his bravery increased his size. His suit of armor, made of leather body armor, had a big "D" on the chest, in royal blue. His

[41]

weapon of choice was the feared blade Leviathan, but he also kept a battle axe handy, just in case. The axe, which had a fiberglass body wrapped in latex foam, also had the royal blue "D" on each blade. His shield, known as The Guardian, was made out of fiberglass, coated in latex, and finished off with Kevlar around the edges.

The shoulders of his armor were elevated to protect his head, and his helmet, with its horizontal eye slit, gave him excellent visibility.

Freddy was the thief. Because Freddy was on the small side, it was easy for him to sneak into an opposing army's camp and steal their battle supplies. Or kidnap their king. Freddy wore a dark green hood, dirty brown vest, with a dark green shirt underneath. His boots were typical medieval boots made of soft leather, and he was armed with a bow and arrow, as well as daggers and a small blade. He carried a small pouch, attached to his belt, which contained balls that exploded into a cloud of smoke on contact. If he got into a jam, Freddy would slam the balls to the ground, the smoke would erupt, and he would disappear.

Jen was, in her words, a "seductress who could thread a needle with a dagger. Oh, and if that doesn't work, I'll just cut your head off with my blade." She wore a leather one-piece outfit, with a short skirt and a low cut top. A red cape and a tiara complimented her outfit. Jen was armed with a belt of daggers and a small knife. The knife had a hard rubber handle, wrapped in leather. The blade itself was fiberglass, covered in latex, with a Kevlar tip. Jen's appearance, and costume, could be a distraction. When she was in costume, she walked with confidence, knowing that she could fight her way out of any situation. Jen wasn't afraid to use her femininity on the battlefield, either. She was always amused at how easily a male opponent would succumb to her charms, moments before she stuck a dagger through his heart.

Mark was a sorcerer. Since he was a total immersionist, he went all out in both costume and in his acting during a battle. His long purple robe was covered in multi-colored cubic zirconia stars which formed a "V" in the middle of the robe for his character Vollrath. No one knew who Vollrath was, or what the name meant, and Mark wouldn't tell anyone. Whenever he put on the robe, he was Vollrath. His hat was also covered in multi-colored cubic zirconia.

After they were dressed, they met in the lobby to wait for the rest of their team. The Verona faction was 30 strong, and was part of a larger LARP group, known as the Kingdom Of Hotzenbella, which was headquartered in central Washington State. The entire Hotzenbella Kingdom only met in person at LARP events, and kept in touch mostly through email.

"That's a really sweet wizard's costume, where did—" Jen began asking Mark.

"I'm not a wizard," Mark said.

Jen looked at Mark, quizzically. "Then what are you?"

"I am an ancient and mighty sorcerer," Mark replied, curtly.

"What's the difference?" Jen asked, a bit defensive.

"How long have you been doing this, now?" Mark responded, disgusted. He continued as if he were explaining a simple concept to a child. "A wizard can read a spell book and cast a spell," Mark said, condescension in his voice. "There's no glory in that. A sorcerer, especially one as old and powerful as me, has the power within him to put forth supernatural destruction few have ever seen. I don't need to memorize a spell. I am the power."

Dennis, still a bit mad over Mark's outburst at breakfast, joined the conversation. "Yeah, but a sorcerer only has a few spells they can do at one time. What have you got, like five, maybe? You can only memorize so many. A wizard can cast as many spells as are in his spell book."

"But my spells are stronger, because they come from within me, see?" Mark retorted.

"I dunno. I'd rather be a wizard." Dennis shrugged, grinning at Jen.

"What do you know, anyway? For starters, you don't even—"

"Hey, you guys ready to get medieval?" said a voice coming

up the hallway. It was Joe Peacock, Hotzenbella King. He looked a lot better than he had a few hours earlier at breakfast. Joe was dressed in a royal purple vest with white trim. Matching purple knickers and tights went with his outfit, and a blindingly shiny gold crown, adorned with a row of twinkling jewels. His long flowing cape was multi-colored to represent his namesake. He carried a long, gold scepter topped with a glass, multi-colored globe. Inside the removable globe was a dagger, which he could use in the event an opposing army tried to capture him.

"Sweet crown, Joe. Is it new?" Freddy asked.

"New to me. Got it on E-LARP right before I left," he said with a smile.

The rest of the Hotzenbella kingdom, the ones staying at Eiler's (some did stay on the battlefield), around fifteen people, showed up in the lobby. Scattered among the army were warriors, knights, warlocks, servants, and blacksmiths. Mark gathered them all in a circle, stood in the middle, and spoke.

"Okay. I'm the GM for today's battle against Oakmont. For those of you who were here last year, you'll remember that they made us look like a bunch of amateurs out there. We lost a lot of people that day, and we lost them fast. This year will be different, I promise."

"How's it gonna be different?" someone asked in the back of the circle.

"It will, trust me," he replied. "Now, here's the back story, which was agreed upon with the GM of Oakmont. Our fair King Peacock has had an affair with the Oakmont Queen."

"Mark, that's nuts. I'd never do that," Joe objected.

"Well, you did. Deal with it. Anyway—"

"Now, hold on a second." Joe's voice deepened. "There is no way I would ever do something like that. I know this is just a role-play, but I'm the character here, and I have a say in what I do. And I would never, ever—"

"You're wrong, again, and as usual," Mark shot back, "I'm the GM, not you. I have the say, not you. While you're chasing kids around a high school, I'm at home working on this stuff. If you don't like what's going on here, there's the door. It doesn't take any talent to be a King. All you gotta do is stay alive. Now, do you think you can handle that?"

The crowd was quiet. Mark had gone too far. Joe was a well-respected member of the Hotzenbella Kingdom. He was a very moral person, with a wife and three daughters, and played his characters with the same degree of morality. Mark's actions would not sit well with the rest of the group. Joe stormed off to the parking lot, with his faction behind him.

"Anyway," Mark continued, oblivious to the angry glares he was getting from his own team, "Joe had his royal way with the Oakmont Queen, and now the King of Oakmont wants revenge. He will accept either the town of Verona or King Peacock's head as payment for the insult. Of course, as we are not in Verona, we will be given a portion of land to defend that represents Verona. I will be guiding the action as we go along, adding pieces of the story to the battle. Please remember to stay in character at all times, don't hit the enemy too hard, keep your hits at a 45 to 90 degree angle, respect the pre-spell counting of wizards and sorcerers, and none of you are immortal . . . if you get hit, go down. Questions?"

A young woman in the circle raised her hand and said, "I just find it offensive that females are used as objects in this story. Couldn't you find a better use for the Oakmont Queen than as a sex object who triggers a war?"

Mark bristled at her comment. He took a deep breath. "Do you follow politics at all? Do you ever watch the news? Don't you know that this stuff happens all the time, and has, forever and ever? This is a storyline that reflects the past in its physical manifestation, yet is a timeless theme. Sometimes women wreck kingdoms. Besides, the Oakmont Queen is a LARP Queen. You know how many times she's tried to lure Hotzenbella subjects away from the kingdom? Have you seen the slutty costumes that woman wears? Did you hear about her and the Warlock from Brooklyn Park? This storyline was bound to happen. Anyone else?"

Jen shook her head, disgusted. "And he wonders why I'm not interested in him," she grumbled to Freddy, who was standing nearby.

With no further questions, the Hotzenbella Kingdom dispersed to their cars for the short drive to the battlefield. .

CHAPTER 6

That afternoon, as Dennis drove to the battlefield, he seriously considered driving straight back to Verona, skipping the battle, and the remaining weekend activities. There was a feeling in his gut that Mark was going to become his usual, unreasonable self, and that he, Dennis, would end up leaving, on the spot. Dennis didn't want to be forever remembered as a quitter at his very last war game. However, the aggravation of dealing with Mark might outweigh any label that would be placed upon him by the rest of the Hotzenbella kingdom. Plus, he'd probably never see these people again, so their opinions didn't matter.

As he drove, he rehearsed two scenarios in his head: the first one was a conversation . . . more like a yelling monologue . . . that he would have with Mark once things went badly on the battlefield. The monologue included telling Mark that he wished he never saved him that day in gym class, and that he had wasted his time and money LARPing with him all these years.

The second scenario was the celebration and hugs that would happen, once they won their battle. They had been preparing for a long time to win the war game in Uniontown, and a victory would be a milestone in their lives and in their friendship. A great way for Dennis to retire. If this were a western LARP, he'd ride off into the sunset, as everyone waved goodbye.

As he was driving to the battlefield, and contemplating the next few hours, his cell phone rang. It was Brad.

Great.

"Is this Dennis the Wizard? Hey, since you're a wizard, can you cast a spell to make yourself cool? Or at least not as dorky. I'd be happy with that," Brad cracked. Dennis could hear people talking and laughing in the background.

"If this isn't life or death important, I'm hanging up."

"Maybe this will change your mind . . . hold on." Dennis

heard Brad cover the phone, then say "Hey, come over here for a minute," in the background.

"Denny?"

It was a female voice, one he hadn't heard in a long time. Only one person called him Denny.

"Alyssa?" Dennis asked, in disbelief.

"Yep, it's me! How are ya?" Her voice sent an electric shock through Dennis's system. He'd thought about her so many times over the years, and hearing her voice now made his heart thunder in his chest.

It made him feel alive.

"I-I-I'm . . . great," Dennis stuttered. He was afraid to ask the next question, but he had to do it. "Are you . . . you're in Verona?"

"Yep, I'm back for a few days, visiting everyone. I rounded up some of the high school gang and came to the Rivertowne for a few drinks, when who walks in but your brother." Dennis could hear her smiling. She sounded happy to be with the old gang. Happy to be home.

"Wow, imagine that. Brad at the Rivertowne," Dennis said, sarcastically. Brad practically lived at the Rivertowne. He always had a captive audience there.

"Well, yeah, Brad's here, but I'd really like to see you. It's been so long, why don't you come down?"

Dennis felt his heart sink, as if the wind had been knocked out of him. It was the past happening all over again. He didn't know what to say.

"You there, Denny?"

Her voice sounded the same. Rich and warm, like a fine scotch. "Yeah, yeah I'm here," Dennis replied, trying to mask his despondency.

"So are you coming to throw a few back with us, or are you too old for the Rivertowne?"

Dennis sighed heavily. "I'd love to, Alyssa, but I can't. I'm in Uniontown."

"Oh . . . Uniontown? What are you doing there? Wait, isn't that where you used to go to those LARK festivals?"

"LARP . . . yeah, I'm here with Mark and Freddy. I'm driving to a war game right now."

"Wow, that's great that you still keep in touch with those guys."

"Yeah, it's great," Dennis said, trying not to sound defeated.

"Oh, well, it was great talking to you, anyway. I'll be here until Monday morning, so if you make it back in time, give me a call. Maybe we can meet for coffee. If not, I should be back sometime within the next year or so."

"Yeah, yeah, great talking to you, too." Dennis couldn't believe it. How could this happen to him twice in the same lifetime?

"Hold on, Brad wants to say goodbye. Here, Brad . . ."

"Hey, Sir Warlock," Brad said in a hushed, mischievous tone, "you oughta see this chick. She hasn't aged a day since high school. There can't be any gravity in Pittsburgh, because everything on her is like a good fastball . . . high and tight."

"Just don't even talk to me," Dennis was about to hang up on Brad, but Brad had one more stake to drive through Dennis's heart. "Look, bro, Alyssa will be fine here without you. Don't worry, The Brad is gonna take this one all the way to the end zone!!! He . . . could . . . go . . . all . . . the . . . wa—"

Dennis hung up angrily and threw his phone in the back seat. There was nothing more for him to say, and nothing more for him to think, because he had said it all, and thought it all.

For years.

His life was what it was. He tried to get the vision of Brad and Alyssa out of his mind. But the more he thought about it, the more vivid the vision became, until he could almost hear Brad trying to impress Alyssa with the same old high school stories. He could see Alyssa playfully rolling her eyes, falling for Brad's brand of charm.

Going home wasn't an option. Not until Alyssa went back to Pittsburgh. How could he go back home to Verona and listen to Brad gloat about his latest conquest? Alyssa was more than a beautiful face; she represented what could have been. What should have been.

[49]

Dennis's greatest fear was that he was right where he was supposed to be in life.

Maybe this was all he had.

Maybe this was all there was.

He decided that he would fulfill his LARP duties, keep to himself, and maybe stay in Uniontown until Alyssa went back to Pittsburgh. After that, Brad wouldn't be a part of his life anymore. Dennis would go home and erase Brad and Alyssa from his memory. He would trudge on through life until he came up with a better plan.

Perhaps it was time for him to leave Verona. With his education and experience, he could easily get a job on the mainland. Or, why not another state? Even another country was an option. Canada is just like America, but colder, he'd heard. He had been in Verona his entire life, and it was all he knew. There had to be more out there for him, away from Brad, and Alyssa's memory. He could go out, live somewhere else, and be free from his—and Verona's—history.

Pulling into the battlefield parking lot, Dennis saw LARPers milling around, preparing for the day's activities. The afternoon sun shone brightly in the clear blue sky. A friendly breeze captured the familiar smell of grilled pork and beef, floating the scent around to everyone. Some of the LARPers remained authentic and grilled on a spit. Others used portable grills. Everyone had their own way of embracing the LARP culture. Teams were helping each other get into costumes, and some were practicing battle formations. Groups were standing in huddles going over strategy. The Hotzenbella kingdom had their own designated spot in the parking lot for one final session.

"Okay, so everybody knows the plan, right? We're to go and capture the king and the queen, if we can. And remember to protect Peacock. His Royal Guards should maintain a circle around him at all times, and should not break the circle," Mark announced to the group. "Are there any questions?"

"Yeah, uh, who's the healer today? I don't remember you going over that at the hotel," one of the Hotzenbella LARPers asked.

"There is no healer today. Any other questions?" Mark shot out.

There was silence in the group. Everyone knew that, without a healer, the army was doomed.

"Wait a minute," Freddy interjected, "What do you mean there's no healer?"

Mark looked at Freddy, perplexed. "I mean there's no healer. I can't make it any simpler than that."

Freddy's jaw clenched. His famous intensity surfaced as he replied to Mark's arrogance.

"How can there not be a healer? What were you thinking? You mean I practiced for months, drove all the way out here, and as soon as I get hit, I'm done?"

Mark tried to answer Freddy's question in a way that made it sound like he actually cared what Freddy thought. "We don't have a healer because I've mastered some really great spells that will prevent any of you from getting hurt. I promise all of you that no one will get killed or hurt today. I'll be watching over everyone."

Dennis looked at the sky, as if he were praying a bolt of lightning would incinerate Mark. When it didn't happen, he exploded, "Are you kidding me? That is the height of stupidity and arrogance. It's like having a football team without a quarterback."

Mark fired back, "So you're Brad now? You relate everything to football?"

Dennis clenched his fists and began walking menacingly toward Mark. Jen intercepted him, put her arm around his waist, and turned him in the opposite direction.

"C'mon, over here. Just relax," she said, soothingly.

They walked toward a tree about thirty feet from the group. Dennis unloaded on Jen

"You know, Alyssa called me on the way over here. She's in Verona right now and wanted me to come to the Rivertowne and hang out. She sounded so good, so happy. Just hearing her voice made me happy, and I haven't been happy in weeks. But guess what? Brad is there, too, and he got on the phone and assured me

[51]

that he would 'take care of' Alyssa for me."

Jen winced in sympathy.

"This is really the last place on earth I want to be right now, and that idiot over there isn't making it any better for me."

Dennis's gaze was fixed on Mark, who was still speaking, as Jen tried to talk Dennis out of leaving.

"We all know there's something wrong with Brad," she said, stating the obvious. "But, do you really think that Alyssa would have anything to do with him? She's had some success in life and has been all over the world. She knows Brad's type, and I can promise you that nothing is going to happen between them. It's not high school anymore. He may be The Brad to all of them, 'cause they never left Verona. But to Alyssa, he's just a loser living on his past glories."

"Do you think?" Dennis said, looking to Jen for validation.

"I know. I'm a woman, trust me," Jen said with a smile.

Jen's assurances about Alyssa helped him to compose himself, and Mark's self-centered behavior made it official: today would be Dennis's last LARP event. He headed to the circle, standing in the back, figuring that everyone in front of him would be able to protect Mark in the event he decided to charge and behead his illustrious GM.

"Okay, we're gonna be stationed near the bottom of that hill over there." Mark pointed to a hill off in the distance. "I will be moving amongst you . . ." he demonstrated this by weaving in and out of the group, "to make sure that no one is in danger of getting maimed or killed."

"I got a question," another Hotzenbella subject spoke up. "What happens if you get maimed or killed?"

Everyone was silent. Mark thought for a minute. "Don't worry, it's not gonna happen."

"What if it does?"

"It's not."

"But what if you get killed?"

"I won't."

"Okay, but just say that it—"

"It's not going to happen!" Mark yelled, glaring at the

questioner.

Dennis and Freddy just looked at each other in disbelief. Everyone in the group was getting impatient with Mark's attitude. Freddy knew that this was it, that Dennis was gone after today. If he even made it through today.

An announcement came over the PA system.

"Attention, everyone. Welcome to the Annual Uniontown KNEL Festival. Attendance has increased thirty-seven per cent from last year, and on behalf of the KNEL Board of Directors, I would like to say thank you." A weak applause fluttered through the crowd. "Now, the first battle of the day in our round robin tournament is about to begin. Remember, the first place prize this year is the coveted KNEL trophy, which will give your army bragging rights for being the best trained, and most feared, LARP army on the West Coast, and possibly the entire country."

This time, the crowd cheered loudly. There was excitement in the air, and everyone was ready to go.

"The first battle of the day is between the Hotzenbella Kingdom of Verona and the army of Oakmont. Armies, please report to your designated areas."

Mark led the march to the hill. Freddy, Dennis and Jen followed at the back of the group. There was a feeling of defeat among the Hotzenbella Army. Only Mark saw victory in the day.

"I feel like we're walking into a lion's den," Freddy said.

"That's 'cause we are," Dennis replied.

"C'mon, guys, it's not that bad. So what if we lose. It's not like we've never lost. We lose, go back to the hotel, have some beers, and live to fight another day," Jen said, trying to cheer up the group.

"That's not the point," Dennis said, frustrated, not looking at Jen as he spoke. Jen shot a look of concern at Freddy, who shook his head in disgust.

The Hotzenbella Kingdom took their places near the bottom of the hill. The Oakmont Army stood at the top. The afternoon sun was behind them, and its light made the armor of the Oakmont Army appear to glow.

The Oakmont king came to the front of the army and

[53]

addressed the Hotzenbella kingdom.

"Hotzenbella Kingdom, your king has corrupted our long standing peace treaty by violating my wife, the fair queen. As payment for this horrid offense, we will accept your Kingdom, or the head of your king."

As was the procedure, Joe Peacock, the King of Verona, stepped forward to respond to the charges. But Mark cut in front of him, and shouted back, "The queen is a bow-legged sow of a woman, who's been seducing Hotzenbella men for years. If you want Peacock's head, come 'n get it!"

Joe Peacock angrily put his hand on Mark's shoulder, spinning him around. "What are you doing? I'm the king. It's my job to respond. You know that!"

The Oakmont king, realizing that protocol had been broken, laughed at Mark's arrogance. It showed disorganization within the Hotzenbella army.

"Fine then, you have sealed your fate," The King shouted back at Mark. "Oakmont, bring me the head of Peacock!!!"

The Oakmont army roared, and charged down the hill, as the Hotzenbella Kingdom took a defensive stance. .

CHAPTER 7

King Peacock was protected by his Royal Guard about twenty yards from where the battle was taking place. The guards carried multicolored shields to represent the great Peacock. They surrounded him, weapons in hand, ready to take anyone who posed a threat to The King.

From his view, King Peacock could see huge axes, swords, shields, and even mallets, swinging wildly. Mark was hunched over, darting in and out of the battle. When it looked like a Hotzenbella member was about to get killed, Mark would magically appear, raise his arms, shout something unintelligible, and the opponent would fall. It was almost as if Mark was operating on some sort of supernatural power. Whenever there was a problem, Mark would materialize.

"Maybe this is going to work," Peacock said to his guards.

"We're prepared for the worst, sire," one of them answered.

In the thick of the battle, Freddy and Dennis were back to back, fighting off an attack from two ogres. Freddy was using Dennis's double-edged sword and Dennis was using Freddy's axe. Dennis was happy in the moment, battling the ogres as if he were battling Mark. Mark showed up to help, fearing that Freddy and Dennis would be killed. When Dennis saw Mark, he cut his enemy in half, spun around, ducked down, and cut off Freddy's enemy at the knees. Saying nothing, Dennis stood up and glared at Mark. Mark knew what he was thinking, and quickly darted away.

The battle raged throughout the field. Despite the episode with Mark, and the deflated feeling it had caused, Verona was dominating Oakmont. Clusters of Hotzenbella allies were saluting each other after every victory. They were working together, as a team, not a collection of individuals.

As Dennis wasted another Oakmont foe, he heard Mark, terrified, calling him. "Den-gar! Den-gar!!"

Dennis quickly disposed of his enemy, and found Mark in the corner of the hill surrounded by six hulking members of the Oakmont army.

"Crap," he said under his breath.

Running at full speed, Dennis overpowered the nearest Oakmont foe. When the Oakmont six saw Den-gar coming, they charged Mark, eager to take him out. Within seconds, Mark was lying in the grass, defeated.

Then they turned on Dennis. He couldn't believe that he had to take on six enemies because of Mark's stupidity. Of all people! It honestly wouldn't have made much of a difference to Dennis if he had said to Mark, "Forget it, I'm busy. Dig yourself out." It would have served Mark right, after all. But Dennis was a warrior, and a team player. He did the only thing he could do— took a defensive stance and fought bravely.

Dennis quickly disposed of three of them, but there were still three more. As he pounded two of them, he felt a blow to the back of his knee, which signaled that his leg had been cut in two. He was forced to fall to the ground, where the enemy immediately "speared" Dennis through the heart.

He "died," according to the rules, and then headed over to where Mark was lying. Dennis raised his axe to the sky, and the blade came crashing down inches from Mark's head. The force was so great that the axe snapped off at the handle. Dennis took what was left of the handle and angrily whipped it into the nearby woods.

"What is your problem?" Mark yelled.

"*You* are my problem!" Dennis screamed back, pointing menacingly at Mark. "You don't bring a healer? What's wrong with you?"

"My spell didn't work on the last group. I couldn't remember all of it. I . . . froze up when I saw them . . . and forgot . . ." Mark trailed off.

"Yeah, well, I got my own spell, and I'm gonna use it to forget you and this whole stupid LARP thing. I'm outta here."

Dennis gave Mark one last menacing look and angrily walked off the battlefield toward his car.

Realizing what had just happened, Mark stood up, expecting Dennis to come to his senses. Dennis continued to walk, with determination, to the parking lot, as Mark slammed his hat to the ground.

Freddy and Jen both saw what was happening and they ran after Dennis, leaving the battlefield.

"Dennis, what's going on?"

"C'mon, man, don't leave!"

"What's going on is that Mark is a delusional moron. He doesn't get it. He doesn't care about anyone else, or the time we've put into this. But the truth is, I've been sick of the whole LARP thing for a while. Mark just made me realize where I should be and what I should be doing. If I could take back all the years I spent on these stupid LARP trips with him, I would," Dennis shouted.

"C'mon, Dennis," Freddy tried to reason. "It hasn't been all bad."

Dennis, realizing that he had just hurt the wrong person, turned to face Freddy and Jen. He was still angry, but his anger was now directed at the right person.

"I'm sorry, you're right. It hasn't been all bad. But I just can't take him anymore and I don't want to spend any more time LARPing, because LARP to me means Mark. So I'm done. I'm leaving."

"I understand," Freddy said, defeated.

"Can you just stay for the rest of the weekend and hang out?" Jen asked, meekly.

"No, this is it. Den-gar is dead. He was slaughtered because of Mark's ego. I'll see you guys back home."

Dennis threw his weapons in the trunk of his car, took off his armor, and sped off.

It was a liberating moment for Dennis, yet it was still painful to leave. He was leaving a part of himself back in Uniontown, leaving the LARP world, and heading into a new world. Dennis did have many good, but stressful, times in that little town. It wasn't LARP that meant so much to him; it was the bonding experience with his friends. Over the years, their friendships grew during their LARP outings, but LARPing with Mark had stretched the bounds of friendship too far, and they snapped.

He was finally free of Mark's LARP obsession, but he had left the team, his friends, to finish out the weekend. It wasn't just a team, it felt more like a family, good people you saw once a year at a reunion or a holiday gathering. Dennis loved the familiarity of going to LARP events because he got to see his "family" and it felt like going home. But, like any family gathering, it sometimes got ugly.

Deep down inside, off and on for years, he had wanted to be free of LARP, and of Mark. He often wondered if he would have been better friends with Mark had LARP not been involved. Something came over Mark whenever LARP was involved. Normally, Mark was the joker of the bunch, very easy going, goofy and playful. He spent most of his time playing guitar in his room (he was in a local prog-rock band called Camelot), buying and selling retro sci-fi/fantasy toys online, or working on LARP-related tasks, like writing new battle stories, or researching the latest advancements in LARP battle gear.

But when it got time to hunker down and start making concrete plans with the rest of the team about a battle, or once the battle actually went down, Mark would transform into an egotistical maniac. Dennis and Freddy talked about it on the side for many years, and they came to the conclusion that LARP was the only thing in Mark's life where he could feel superior to someone else. He was a college drop-out, who lived in his parents' attic, and sold toys for a living. Dennis, Freddy, and Jen all had successful jobs, and bright professional futures. Mark was still doing the same things he'd done when he was fourteen. No one in the group judged him, but it was clear that Mark judged himself.

Dennis decided to head home, back to Verona. Alyssa was still there, and maybe Jen was right. Maybe Alyssa saw Brad as a loser, still drinking, at the Rivertowne, on his high school football years. Maybe all the things that Dennis wished and thought about over the years would come true this weekend. Alyssa still thought about him. Her phone call made it obvious.

Their conversation made it clear that Pittsburgh hadn't changed her at all. She still sounded like the same unassuming, genuine girl from Verona that he'd known his entire life.

As Dennis headed back to Verona, driving west on Route 20, he let out a deep sigh, set his eyes on the horizon, and drove. He would drive to the edge of the mainland, cross the Hulton Bridge, and be back in Verona by dusk. His future was ahead of him, his past was behind him, and peace was in his heart.

Two hours later, Dennis arrived at the Hulton Bridge. There was a long, long line to go across the bridge, and Dennis could see police lights near the bridge entrance.

Great, I'm finally going to right this wrong in my life, and try to make up with Alyssa, and someone decides to wreck their car right at the bridge entrance. He changed the CD in his car, sat back, and tried to relax.

Five minutes passed.

Then ten.

Dennis checked his cell phone, and there was a text from Freddy.

"Sucks here without you," said the message. "Mark wants to patch things up when we get home." Dennis shook his head, partially in disgust at Mark's behavior, and partially because he knew Mark would try to make amends. He was still incensed, and didn't want to think about a future that had anything to do with Mark. The only future that mattered was one that he dreamt about with Alyssa.

After fifteen minutes, cars started turning around to go the other way. Dennis was able to get closer to the bridge. Blocking the entrance were several enormous military Humvees, face to face, and lots of local and state police. Blue and red lights lit up the dusk sky, and heavily armed soldiers were milling around the bridge.

Cars turned around in droves, as a stern looking soldier waved everyone in the opposite direction of the bridge. He was determined to protect the bridge, and looked as if he would do whatever it took to keep people away from the entrance. Dennis, surprised and confused by the whole scene, parked his car at a

Mauro's gas station, and walked up to a nearby soldier who was speaking with the local police.

"Um, excuse me, sir, what's going on?" Dennis asked politely.

"You can't cross the bridge," the soldier said, turning to look at Dennis. When he saw that Dennis wasn't a threat, he continued. "We've set up a detour. Please turn around and follow the signs," the soldier turned to face the police again, and resumed his conversation.

"Why can't I cross the bridge? Is there a problem with it?"

The soldier turned again, surprised to see that Dennis was still there.

"Yes".

Dennis expected a detailed answer from the soldier, but it was clear that the soldier wasn't interested in volunteering information to a civilian.

"So . . . what's the problem?" Dennis persisted.

"I'm not at liberty to discuss it. Just follow the detour."

The soldier turned around again, expecting Dennis to leave.

Dennis, still a little angry at the day's events, forcefully asked, "Detour to where? I live in Verona and the only way to get there is across this bridge. What do you want me to do, swim there?"

The soldier snapped back, "I don't care *what* you do! But you can't cross this bridge. Take the detour and get out of hereDennis didn't back down. "I am a U.S. citizen and I've lived in Verona my whole life. My family has lived there for more than fifty years, and they are still there. If I can't cross this bridge to get home, I demand to know why."

The soldier's face turned red, and he got nose to nose with Dennis. He answered in a low, menacing tone, "I don't have to tell you anything. You should be glad that you're still here. I could easily have you hauled off . . . or shot. How do I know you're not one of *them*?"

One of who? Dennis thought, as the stare-down continued. Neither man was giving up. As the tension rose, a voice came from the crowd of military men.

"Stand down, soldier."

The soldier suddenly stood erect with his hands to his side. It was like a switch was flipped in his brain. "Yes, sir!"

An older military man approached Dennis, as the younger soldier walked away. "I am Lieutenant Richards. How can I help you?"

"I don't want to cause a problem, sir," Dennis answered, regaining his composure "I live in Verona and I just want to know why I can't go home."

"Well, the truth is that you can't go home because about half of the bridge has been destroyed."

Dennis looked at Richards in disbelief. "What?"

"Yes, the bridge is out of commission, so you will need to find other accommodations. I understand that this is the only bridge to Verona, but there's nothing we can do right now."

"What do you mean 'destroyed'? Do you mean that the bridge had some sort of engineering problems, and it collapsed?" Dennis asked in shock.

"No, it has been destroyed," Richards answered, factually.

"By . . . what? Who?" Every word that came out of Dennis's mouth came out weaker and weaker. He felt like he was watching this conversation happen, as opposed to being a part of it.

"We don't know. But it looks like whoever destroyed Verona has also taken it."

"Taken? Taken where? Where did it go?" Dennis was trying to hold his emotions together, and was losing the battle with each answer that Richards provided.

"It's not a matter of where. It looks as though an army has come, destroyed the end of the bridge that is closest to Verona, and taken the land, and its citizens, hostage." Richards sounded like he was reading a news report.

Dennis looked at Richards in disbelief. This had to be a joke. At any moment he expected Brad to jump out of a bush and holler "got ya! That's what you get for going to the Nerd-a-palooza in Uniontown!!!"

Dennis was silent for a few seconds. Richards, sensing that

Dennis was worried about his family, changed his tone. "I'm sorry, that's all I can tell you," he said with all the military compassion he could muster. "The best thing for you to do is to find a hotel, stay there, and watch the news. When this situation is over, we'll alert the media so that everyone can go home."

Dennis took out his cell phone to call Brad. He couldn't believe he was actually calling Brad.

"That's not going to work," Richards said. "They've destroyed the cell phone tower in Verona, along with the entire infrastructure that handles electricity."

Dennis looked at Richards as if Richards were speaking a foreign language. "Thank you for the information." Dennis walked back to his car, in a daze. .

CHAPTER 8

As Dennis followed the detour route in disbelief, he remembered the pharmacy that bordered on the river overlooking Verona. He pulled into the pharmacy parking lot, got out of his car, and went to his trunk, where he kept a telescope in there for scouting missions during LARP battles. If Verona was on its last legs, he had to know. Dennis grabbed the long, white telescope, and, cautiously, looked over his shoulder. Now would be an absolutely awful time to get arrested by the military police. When he saw that the MP was occupied, he raced to the back of the pharmacy, which faced Verona.

Dennis closed his eyes, took a deep breath, exhaled, opened his eyes, and slowly raised the telescope to his right eye. Gradually, he adjusted the lens, bringing the island sharply into view. It was dusk now, and night would be coming soon. Verona was blanketed in darkness, except for patches of yellowish red dots that covered the island—bonfires. Burning plastic and gasoline gripped Dennis's throat, and his entire body coughed. If death had an odor, this was it.

He scanned the island through his telescope. The end of the Hulton Bridge on the Verona side was mangled, and drowning, in the Strait of Georgia. The bright neon light that always glowed from the huge pair of cherry-red lips perched atop the Kiss beverage plant had been snuffed out. Verona's tallest structure, the cell phone tower, had vanished, along with the smaller towers at the power plant.

The normal signs of everyday life on Verona were nowhere to be seen. The island looked as it did hundreds of years ago, before it was inhabited.

Dennis had visions of his family and friends being tortured, or worse. What if Brad got killed trying to play the hero? Dennis didn't always agree with Brad, and most of the time he didn't even like him, but they were brothers. What if he was . . . gone?

He wondered if his house was still there—the house that his grandparents had bought when they were his age, and had lived in for more than fifty years. The house where his mother grew up. The house his grandparents left him in their will. That house meant more to him than its physical value; it meant family to him. It meant three generations, it meant love; it meant struggle and success.

The next scene that filled Dennis's telescope was unbelievable; five wooden battleships docked at the Verona shoreline. The intimidating size of the ships, and the menacing cannon ports, dared any challenge to their authority.

The ships were docked as if they owned Verona. Dennis lowered the telescope, looked again with his naked eye, and saw the same thing, only smaller. He raised the telescope again, and took another look.

Wooden battleships?

Dennis stood in disbelief for a few moments, trying to make sense of the situation. But everything was illogical. The Hulton Bridge was in the water, and wooden battleships were docked at Verona. Police and military covered the area.

He needed to head back to Uniontown.

Dennis sent Freddy a text message saying, "Coming back. Get to the hotel ASAP." He ran to his car, threw the telescope in the back seat, and got back on the road.

Dennis scanned the radio stations while he was speeding down Route 20 East. Every report said the same thing.

Nothing.

None of the usual world terror organizations claimed responsibility for the attack. The general consensus was that a rogue group had taken Verona. A representative from the US Armed Forces was heading to Verona, by boat, to try to establish communication with the invaders. The Red Cross asked permission to visit Verona, to offer medical aid to the citizens.

Of course, conspiracy theorists said the invasion was a sign of the apocalypse. Political commentators claimed that opposing parties were responsible for the lapse in security in Verona. The President, at a press conference, denounced the attack, and said that every effort was being made to bring the invaders to justice.

A big-name political commentator claimed the president was behind the attacks in an effort to boost his sagging approval rating.

Nearly halfway through the drive back to Uniontown, a report came in that the small boat carrying representatives from the Red Cross and US government had been clipped by a cannonball, launched from one of the invading ships. Luckily, everyone was wearing a life jacket, and swam back to the mainland.

Dennis turned off the radio, stepped on the gas, and tried to keep from panicking. .

CHAPTER 9

When he got back to Eiler's Hotel in Uniontown, a large group of people were sitting, and standing, near the big screen TV in the Great Room. Dennis entered the room, and immediately locked eyes with Freddy, Mark and Jen, who were across the room.

He walked up to them, and Mark said to Dennis, "Listen, Dennis, I'm really—"

Dennis put up his hand and said softly, "It doesn't matter now."

Mark was silent and knew that he was forgiven. Some situations cut the fat off of life. This was one of those times. Whatever problems Dennis had with Mark, or LARP, weren't important right now.

There were a few moments of silence, as they watched the coverage, and then Dennis spoke up. "I saw it."

"Saw what?" Freddy asked, knowing and fearing the answer.

"Verona. I saw . . . the whole thing."

"How bad is it?" Jen asked. Even though she wasn't from Verona, she shared their pain.

"It's tough to say what's going on," Dennis continued, "because it's so dark over there. It's just black. Even the Kiss sign is out. Those lips have been lit for as long as I can remember. The only light I could see was from bonfires."

"I heard something about wooden ships?" Mark asked.

"Yeah, I saw them," Dennis answered, still having a hard time processing the image.

"Wooden ships?" Mark asked again.

"Yeah, with sails, masts, and cannon ports. Just like you see in those old pirate movies."

Just then Jen's phone rang. It was her dad. "Yeah, that's a great idea. I'd feel safer, too. Are you sure? Okay, I'll ask them . . . All right, dad, I'll tell them. We'll be there soon.

That was my dad. He wants us to go to Fort Lewis and stay there until this is cleared up. He says it will be the safest place for us, and there's plenty of room."

Freddy, Dennis and Mark looked at each other.

"Seems like we're getting farther and farther away from Verona," Mark observed, with a hint of insecurity.

"I think it's best right now," Freddy agreed.

"Me, too. There's nothing we can do here," Dennis added, slightly homesick.

"Okay, let's get our stuff," Jen said, turning to go to her room. Freddy and Mark followed.

Dennis got closer to the TV. He had a lump in his throat as he saw Verona from a view of a helicopter on the news. The screen showed bonfires all over the island, and some buildings were on fire.

The reporter said in a matter-of-fact tone, "Anything could be happening down there. We just don't know."

Dennis turned away from the TV, and waited in the parking lot for his friends. .

CHAPTER 10

Jen, Freddy and Mark were silent as they came down the steps, through the great hall, past the crowd, which got bigger by the moment, and out to the parking lot. Dennis was already sitting in his car, with the engine going, waiting for them.

After they packed up their cars, Mark said to Freddy, "I'm gonna ride with Dennis."

Freddy paused, then asked, "Are you sure? It's a few hours to Fort Lewis. That's a long time to sit in silence."

"Yeah, it'll be fine."

Mark timidly knocked on the passenger side window of Dennis's car. The window lowered slowly. "Mind if I ride with you?" Mark asked.

For a minute, the thought of saying "no" occurred to Dennis, but now wasn't the time to be petty. "Sure, man," Dennis replied, trying to sound welcoming.

Jen pulled out and headed for the hotel exit, followed by Freddy, with Dennis and Mark at the rear. It would take a few hours to reach Fort Lewis in Tacoma, by way of Route 5 south. Dennis didn't turn on the radio because he didn't want to hear about what was going on in Verona. He'd seen what was happening. He felt what was happening. He didn't need to listen to a bunch of reporters speculate for the next few hours.

"So look," Mark said, a few minutes into the trip. "I know you said before that it didn't matter, and maybe it doesn't in light of what's going on, but I'm sorry for the way I've been behaving. I don't know what comes over me when it comes to LARP."

Dennis had lots of answers to Mark's open-ended statement, but said nothing.

Mark continued, "It's just . . . I really feel like somebody when I'm doing anything LARP-related. When I'm coming up with a storyline, or researching battle gear or whatever, I'm in control. I'm in control of a whole 'nother universe, a whole 'nother world. It takes me out of my mom's attic to somewhere else. I . . . I don't have much going on. I don't have the same kinda life that you and Freddy have. But I have LARP, and at least I can be in control of that. I know that I can get carried away, but your friendship means more to me than pretty much anything. I hope we can still be friends, but if we can't, then—"

"Look, it's fine," Dennis said, cutting him off, while still being kind. "I know who you are, and I know what LARP makes you. You're a good person, but you've really gotta make some changes. The way you treated Joe Peacock today was embarrassing. I was embarrassed for you, and for us. We're still friends, but I'm done LARPing for a while."

"I understand. Our friendship is more important. And I feel horrible about what I said to Joe. Especially with what's going on now. LARP doesn't seem as important. I'm gonna make things right with Joe, and everyone, I promise," Mark eagerly responded.

Darkness had set it and the streetlights along Route 5 went on forever. "I wonder sometimes about all the people who've driven past these same lights," Mark said gazing out the window. "These lights have been here forever. Fifty years, at least. Where were all those people going? Did they ever get there? Were they disappointed when they arrived?"

"That's kinda like life, isn't it?" Dennis answered. "We're in a hurry to get to the next thing, the next phase, and then when we get there, we wish we could go back. Sometimes I don't know what's more important—where I've been, where I am, or where I'm going."

"I think where you've been is the most important, 'cause it leads you to where you are and where you're going," Mark replied, still studying the lights.

"Yeah, but we change along the way," Dennis said. These were the kind of conversations Mark and Dennis used to have before LARP became the focus of their friendship. The conversation felt good, familiar.

"I'm not who I was five years ago, and I wonder what makes

people change along the way. What makes us choose the roads we take? Guess it's our experiences," Dennis concluded.

"That, and how we see ourselves. I think we act the way we see ourselves, whether our reality is true or not," Mark commented.

"Ever notice how it looks like the streetlights attach themselves to your car? It looks like they attach to the windshield and whip you to the next light," Dennis observed.

"Huh . . . never thought about that," Mark replied. He, too, knew that it was conversations like this that partially helped to build their friendship. Conversations about nothing that meant everything.

"So, how do you think I'm doing with Jen this weekend? I think there've been a few small victories here and there," Mark asked, half-joking.

"No comment," Dennis replied with a smile. "But you better not try anything at Fort Lewis with her dad around. I'm sure he could see to it that you're instantly drafted and sent to Siberia."

"Do they still send people there?" Mark asked, quizzically.

"Who knows? But I'm sure they'd make an exception in your case."

"Huh."

They finally arrived at Fort Lewis, and pulled into the parking lot of the Fort Lewis Inn, a big hotel on the Fort Lewis compound. Cars were parked, bags unloaded, and they made their way to the front desk.

"Hi, I'm Jen Cassady. My dad is General Jack Cassady. I believe he has rooms reserved for us."

"Yes, General Cassady is in room 731. You are in room 732, and your friends are in room 733," said the desk clerk.

"Wait . . . we're all in the same room? Why does she get her own room?" Mark asked.

"'Cause I'm the general's little girl," Jen answered with a wink.

Keys were distributed, and everyone headed up to the seventh floor. The elevator door slid open, and Jen's dad was standing there to greet them.

"Daddy!" Jen said, as she embraced her dad.

"Hi, pumpkin," the general said, bending down slightly to hug his daughter. The general was a lifetime military man. His snow-white buzz cut crowned a remarkably youthful face.

"Daddy, this is Dennis, Freddy, and Mark," Jen said, turning to her friends.

"Nice to meet you, sir. Thank you for making these accommodations for us," Dennis said.

"Yes, sir. It was very kind of you," Freddy chimed in.

"It's no problem at all. I want my daughter, and her friends, to be safe." The general noticed that Mark was sullen, and hadn't expressed his thanks. "What's wrong with him?"

"Nothing, he's just—" Jen started

"Are you upset by the accommodations, son?" the general asked Mark.

Mark finally spoke carefully. "Well, no, it's just . . ."

"Oh, I get it," the general said. "You were hoping for your own room, is that it?"

"Well, yeah, I mean—"

"Or maybe something better than your own room. Maybe you could have shared a room with my daughter. Would that have been more to your liking?"

Mark turned pale. "Well . . . I . . . no, of course not . . ."

"Well, let me tell you something, son," the general said, sternly, staring Mark down. "The US Army is filled with guys like you who wanted to share a room with my daughter. And guess what? There's no vacancy there. Got it?"

"Yes, sir," Mark said. He was almost shaking. Freddy, Dennis and Jen exchanged glances. Jen winked at them to let them know that her dad was playfully harassing Mark.

"Now, the rest of you, drop off your stuff and report to my room," the general said, in his military tone.

"Yes, sir," the group responded in unison.

As the general walked away, Dennis saw a smile on General Cassady's face.

"I think he's got your number," Freddy said to Mark, as they headed down the hall.

"I'm not sayin' nothin' the rest of the time we're here. Nothin'," Mark said, seriously.

"I should have invited Dad to Uniontown. It would have saved us a lot of grief," Jen cracked.

The luggage was dropped off, and everyone headed to the general's room.

As they approached the room, they heard the general talking, and a familiar voice responding.

"I just don't see how's it's possible, General. There'll be too many civilian causalities," the voice said.

"Well, then, what can we do? We can't just give up the land. Do you understand that nothing like that has ever happened in US history?" the general responded, his muscular arms crossed.

Dennis looked at Jen. "Should we go in?"

"Yeah, he said he wanted to see us." Jen knocked on the door before entering. "Daddy? It's us."

The door opened, and the general welcomed them into the large room. The room looked like an apartment, with a kitchen, living room, dining room, big screen TV, and two large bedrooms. Sitting in the dining room was a familiar face, one that Jen, Dennis, Mark, and Freddy had seen on TV and in the papers countless times.

"Come in, honey," said the general. "I want you to meet someone. Governor Serling, this is my daughter Jen, and her friends Dennis, Freddy, and Mark."

They went over and shook the governor's hand, exchanging pleasantries. Governor Serling was the governor of the state of Washington. He was a short, intense looking man, in his early 40s, with coal black hair, and bushy eyebrows.

"So," the governor said, "I understand that you live in Verona."

"We do, Governor," Freddy said, indicating himself, Mark and Dennis, "But Jen lives here on the mainland."

"Which one of you actually saw the aftermath of the invasion?" the governor inquired.

"It was me, sir," Dennis said, his voice quivering a bit at the thought of what he saw, and what might be happening in Verona at that very minute.

"Can we speak privately?" the governor asked.

"Yes, absolutely."

"Why don't you go down to the restaurant and have some dinner. We'll join you shortly," the general said to Jen, Freddy, and Mark.

"Okay, Daddy, see you there," Jen said, as they left.

In the background, the big screen TV was on with the local military news channel broadcasting the latest information about the invasion. The governor watched the TV for a moment, as if lost in thought, and the only person in the room. The general walked over to the bar, poured himself a drink, and sat at the table to watch the TV. It seemed like an hour went by, with the three of them staring at the TV, watching history unfolding minute by minute. Dennis secretly hoped that it was only a movie, and that everything would be resolved before the next commercial break. But he knew better.

Governor Serling finally turned to Dennis. "So what did you see?"

"Well, sir . . . um . . . I really don't know what I saw. It was so unreal. I tried to cross the Hulton Bridge, the only bridge that connects the mainland to Verona, and the military guard told me that I couldn't cross because part of the bridge, on the Verona side, was destroyed. There really wasn't much I could do about it, so I followed the detour. But I live in Verona, you know? Verona's been my family home for generations. I couldn't just drive away, like it wasn't happening. So I pulled over at a pharmacy, got out my telescope, went to the back of the building to the side that faces Verona, and tried to see what was going on."

"And what did you see?" Serling's tone was welcoming, but firm.

"I saw . . . nothing. Just blackness. All the lights were out in Verona. All over the island. Even the giant Kiss sign was out, and I've never seen that happen. There were bonfires, big ones, spaced out on the island. I could smell fire, and things burning, but I couldn't quite put my finger on what was burning. It didn't smell like wood or plastic or chemicals, or cement . . . but it did. Sort of like all those things were mixed up and burning. And the smoke was burning my eyes, even though I was on the mainland. Then I saw . . . ships."

"Ships? Do you mean planes or boats?"

"Boats."

"What did they look like?"

"Well, that's just it. I don't know if the smoke burning my eyes made me see them in a way that wasn't . . . real . . . but they looked like old wooden battleships. Like old pirate ships, with cannon portholes and everything."

Governor Serling shook his head, knowingly.

Dennis continued, "How can that be? Nobody's used that type of ship for what . . . like 150 years?"

"Not quite," the general answered, without turning his attention away from the TV.

"So, what's the story, then? Did some evil pirate time travelers come and conquer Verona?" Dennis half-joked.

The general and the governor looked at each other. They weren't sure how much to share with Dennis.

"Well, look, he's not gonna leave the base until it's all over," the general said to Serling, as if he were finishing, out loud, a conversation that began silently, "and he can't contact anyone on the island, because their cell phone towers are down."

Serling took a deep breath, and exhaled. "Okay, Dennis, here's what we know. The invaders are from Mongolia. I just got off the phone with our UN people in Mongolia, and they assured me that this is a rogue group not affiliated with the Mongolian government in any way. From what the UN said, this rogue group left Mongolia because they refuse to conform to twenty-first century living standards. Mongolia has a democratic government similar to ours, but the group that is in Verona wants to turn back the clock to the time of Genghis Kahn. They planned on overthrowing the Mongolian government, so they could make the country into their own medieval paradise. What probably happened is that the government got wind of the plan, the rogue group found out, and left before they were captured."

Dennis shook his head in disbelief. "But isn't Mongolia a landlocked country? They couldn't have set sail from there, right?"

"You're right," Governor Serling said, nodding. "But they have friends in North Korea. Our guess is that the North Koreans funded their trip with the promise that they would be invited to the party once the rogue Mongols took Verona."

"So the Mongols made their way to North Korea and set sail from there?"

"Yes," General Cassady replied.

"Why did they attack Verona? What would they want with such a tiny island?" Dennis probed.

"Independence and money," the general replied. "Verona was an easy target. It's small, like you said, easy to conquer, since it has no army stationed on the island. Verona is accessible from the Pacific Ocean, so the rogue Mongols can earn some easy cash by letting our enemies dock, and plan an American attack, right on our own soil."

"Plus," said Serling, "What this group is looking to do is to conquer an island and turn it into what they think an ideal society should be, since they couldn't do it in Mongolia. Their plan is to stay there and basically turn back the clock about seven or eight hundred years."

"So, they're just gonna take over Verona and stay there?"

Dennis was angry and scared, and Serling could see it. He tried to calm Dennis.

"No, not at all. We're not going to let that happen. In fact, we were just talking about that right before you walked in. See, here's the dilemma. The US Army could easily go in and . . . remove this rogue group. The problem is that our army is so powerful that our sheer force would probably inflict heavy causalities—"

"So what?!" Dennis said, defiantly.

"—on civilians," Serling said, finishing his sentence.

Dennis sat in stunned silence. General Cassady stepped in to soften the reality.

"Look, Dennis, we know what we have to do. We just don't

know how to do it, yet. Our army is trained and equipped to take on countries, not rogue armies of a few hundred men. If we went in there now, it would be like killing an ant with a cannon."

"I understand," said Dennis, quietly.

"Look, from what we know," Serling continued, "These aren't the same type of people who took down the World Trade Center. While they are dangerous, they're not over there killing everyone. What they're probably doing is destroying a lot of infrastructure, which is why there's no electricity or cell phone service. Destroying all the modern stuff makes sense to them, because they're trying to turn back the clock."

"So, what's next?" Dennis asked, defeated.

"Well, we're consulting with our military team, and with the Mongolian government, who have been extremely cooperative. We're going to try to negotiate with the rogue group to get them out of there, but if that doesn't work, other options will be explored," said the general.

"I know this is difficult for you, and it's tough not to worry," Serling said, doing his best to reassure Dennis, "but we have all of our bases covered. Just try not to worry, and let us handle everything, okay?"

Governor Serling could see that he hadn't convinced Dennis of anything, but Dennis still nodded.

"Go down and meet up with everyone else. Get yourself something to eat, whatever you like. Everything is on me. I'll be down soon," the general said, sounding more like a father than a military commander.

Dennis shook hands with Governor Serling and General Cassady, and then headed to the hotel restaurant.

Once Dennis had left the room, Serling continued the conversation with the general.

"If negotiations don't work, I don't know what we're gonna do. It's a disaster either way." .

CHAPTER 11

It just didn't make sense. The whole scenario was illogical. Like a nightmare.

When Jen, Freddy and Mark saw Dennis enter the restaurant, their expressions changed from worry to expectancy. They wanted the news, and all Dennis wanted was to stop talking about it. The invasion—and that's what it was, an invasion—had been all he had thought about for the last few hours. He just didn't want to think about it anymore. Let the government think about it. That's why he paid taxes.

Dennis sat in his chair and said nothing. The other three looked at each other, puzzled.

"So, what did they say?" Freddy finally asked.

Dennis looked at them for a moment and thought about the most concise way to give out the details.

"A rogue army has taken Verona captive. Their goal is to make the island into their wacko idea of paradise, circa 800 years ago, and to let our enemies in to attack us from our own soil. They've destroyed a lot of infrastructure there, to go along with the whole medieval thing, but no one is too sure what's going on with everyone there."

"Where are they from?" Jen asked.

"Mongolia," Dennis said.

When Freddy heard that the enemy was from the country of his ancestors, he was taken aback.

"Mongolia? Are you sure?"

"That's what they told me. The Mongolian government has even confirmed it."

Freddy, a million questions running through his head, blurted out the nearest one to his lips, "What do they want with us?"

"Like I said, they want to colonize Verona, and help the bad guys attack us. They chose Verona to conquer because it's so small, and it will be easy for our enemies to get to from the Pacific."

"So, what are my dad and the governor going to do about it?" Jen asked.

"Well, they're gonna try to negotiate with them to get them off the island."

"And what if that doesn't work?" Jen questioned. "Then what?"

"They don't know. Your dad told me that the US has too much firepower to go into Verona, that it would destroy the island and everyone on it. It sounds like the military has no idea how to fight a medieval army. There's no training for that."

"So that's it, then? We just wait and hope they leave?" Freddy asked anxiously. He was angry that there wasn't a plan, and angry that his own people, a culture that he was so proud to be a part of, had betrayed him.

Dennis just shrugged his shoulders.

"Guys, listen," Jen said, "I know it's easier for me to say, because I don't live there, but try not to worry too much. My dad has been in a lot of tough situations in his life, and he's always figured a way out. It might not happen tomorrow, but I know that my dad is going to work this out, eventually."

"Eventually? Eventually?!" Freddy snapped at Jen. "While we're sitting here, anything—anything—could be happening to our families. And how long is eventually? Three days? Three years?"

"Look, Freddy, I know how tough it is—" Jen tried to smooth things over.

"No, you don't know how tough it is 'cause it isn't you. Your dad is safe in this hotel, surrounded by tanks and guns. I have no idea where my dad is right now, or if he's even alive."

"Verona might not even be worth saving by the time they do whatever they're gonna do," Dennis said quietly.

"That's our home, Dennis," Freddy said firmly. "That's where our families have lived forever. I will fight for the last twig in Verona. I'm gonna go talk to the general right now and tell him to sign me up. If they're going in to save Verona, I'm going too." Freddy was a fighter at heart. He even looked physically bigger, stronger, than he did earlier in the day.

Just as Freddy threw down his napkin and got up to leave, Mark spoke. He hadn't said anything since Dennis sat down. "We could totally take them."

"Yeah, I know." Dennis started to say, "But the general said that the US has too much—"

"No," Mark interrupted. "We could totally take them. I'm sure of it."

Freddy sat down, his anger on hold. He was intrigued by Mark's comment. "Who's we? The four of us?"

"Yes," Mark said, "and others."

"Stop being so freakin' cryptic and tell us what you mean," Jen insisted.

"We, LARPers, could beat that army."

"At what? A jousting competition?" Freddy asked with a mix of sarcasm and defiance.

Dennis sided with Freddy. "You know what, Mark? Don't even start with me. This is serious stuff, and—"

"Listen to what I'm saying," Mark interrupted. His voice was calm, rational, relaxed. "We've been practicing medieval battle tactics for years. We know every play in the book. What's the difference between what they do and what we do?"

"Well, for starters," Dennis said, sarcastically, "I don't think they're armed with boffer weapons over there, and I'm pretty sure they would kill us without a thought."

"And you wouldn't do the same thing to save your family and your home?" Mark asked in the same level tone. This was a side of Mark that no one had ever seen. He was very confident, but not cocky. It was like he had planned out how to defeat the Mongols before it had even happened.

Freddy adamantly shook his head no. "We're not real warriors. We work desk jobs all week, and run around in the woods with fake weapons on the weekend. We're way out of our element here."

Jen spoke up. "I can't believe I'm saying it, but Mark is kinda right about this. I mean, how else are you going to get your home back?"

"I'm going to let the government handle it. Whatever they say, goes. Freddy's right. We're just a bunch of corporate stooges. We wouldn't last five minutes on a real battlefield," Dennis said logically.

Mark became animated as he offered a retort. "We've been on a real battlefield every single freakin' weekend for the last ten years! We would boot that army out in one day, two days tops. I'm telling ya, as sure as we're sitting here, we would win. We have the experience, we have the training, and we have something real to fight for."

"And we don't have any weapons. Not real ones, anyway," Dennis challenged.

"I've got that all figured out," Mark said slyly.

There was silence as the group studied Mark. Considering the source, the comment could mean anything.

"You go off and get killed. I'm going to our room. I need to lie down." Dennis left the table.

Jen and Freddy looked at Mark. They knew what he was thinking.

"I have to try," he said as he got up and left the table. Jen and Freddy looked at each other for a minute, and followed Mark, as he headed for the elevator.

"You better be sure about this, 'cause my dad isn't gonna like it if you cut in on his time with the governor and make a fool of yourself," Jen shouted to Mark as she chased him down the hallway.

Mark held the elevator door for her and Freddy, and as it closed, he said to Jen, "I am sure about this, but you're gonna come with me, just for insurance."

"What?" Jen said in disbelief. "I don't know. I mean, this is big stuff we're talking about and—"

"And a few short minutes ago, you agreed with me. Your dad will be more apt to listen if you're there, if for no other reason than he won't want to make his princess feel bad, right?"

Looking away, Jen said, "Okay, fine. We've got nothing to lose, anyway."

"Is there anything you want me to do?" Freddy asked.

"Yeah, if the general lunges for me, pull him off," Mark said, half-serious.

The elevator opened and Jen, Mark, and Freddy headed to the general's hotel room. They were nervous, yet had the confidence that they would at least be heard. Before Jen knocked on the door, Mark took out his inhaler, used it, and said, "Okay, let's do it."

Jen knocked on the door. "Daddy, it's us. Do you have a minute?"

The door opened almost immediately, and the general said, "We're kind of in the middle of something here, sweetheart. How important is this?"

Before Jen could answer, Mark spoke up.

"Very, sir."

The general stood back, and they entered the room. Governor Serling was still sitting in the dining area. He was studying a map of Verona. Serling looked up, as Mark headed over to the table, and greeted him warmly.

"Hello, how was lunch?"

"It was fine, sir," Mark said. He was nervous, as he rehearsed the speech to the governor and general in his head. "Do you have a minute? I'd like to talk to you about something."

Serling focused his attention on Mark.

"Governor, General, I think I have a solution to the Verona problem."

Both Governor Serling and General Cassady focused all their attention on Mark. He expected them to say, "What is it?" or "Tell us" or even "Okay" but they said nothing, so he continued.

"Dennis, Jen, Freddy, and I are involved in a Live Action Role Play kingdom, commonly known as LARP, and our era of choice is the medieval period."

Governor Serling spoke up. "LARPers, huh?" said the governor, nodding and smiling. "I used to LARP."

Mark's eyes widened. No one else in the room could believe it.

"You . . . you did?"

"Oh, yeah, went to the KNEL Fest for many, many years. My army was incredibly dominant for about five years. But once I took public office, I had to stop. There just weren't enough minutes in the day to deal with public issues and to stay updated on the best type of weapons."

"Wow!" said Mark, stunned, looking at the others. "Well, sir, if you ever want to get back in, you are certainly welcome to join our army. It would be an honor to battle at your side."

Everyone, with the exception of Mark and the governor, were looking at each other in disbelief. Who knew the governor used to run through the woods of Washington, dressed like a warrior of old?

Mark's excitement had gotten him off topic, but he was more comfortable now that he was talking to a fellow LARPer. He continued.

"Our kingdom covers the island of Verona, plus parts of the mainland. We often go to the Seattle Museum, where Jen works, to do research on medieval battle gear and methods. We became friends with Jen, and she joined our kingdom, the mighty Hotzenbella kingdom. Our kingdom is very well trained in medieval warfare. And it's not only our kingdom, but all the other kingdoms in our league, too. I . . . I don't know how to say it any other way, but we want to battle the Mongols for Verona."

Mark waited for a response.

He didn't get one.

The governor was thinking, but the general's eyebrow was raised, like he thought Mark was totally insane.

Mark took a deep breath and continued.

"Look, you said yourself that the US is not prepared to battle a medieval army, but we are. We've been doing this every weekend for years. We know the battle style. We know the weapons. We know exactly what to do."

The general spoke up, as if talking to someone who was mentally impaired. "Mark, you realize that this is a real situation? These guys aren't playing around. You're not going to just get a scrape on the arm or a pulled hamstring from battling the Mongols."

"Yes, General, we know. I've taken that into consideration, but I don't see any other option for any of us. I agree, the overwhelming force will kill lots of innocent people, and destroy the island. If you don't go in there, or if you wait a long time before going in, lots of people could die just from the Mongols doing who knows what to them. Something needs to be done, and it needs to be done soon. With all due respect . . ."

Meanwhile, Dennis was back in his hotel room, alone, watching the news. There wasn't anything else on TV. Every channel was covering the events in Verona, as if Verona were the center of the universe. Ignoring it wouldn't make it go away, so he watched it unfold.

The media outlets couldn't make it to the island, so all the video footage of the invasion was shot by helicopter. And even that footage was disappearing, because of all the smoke emanating from the island. That, and the cannonballs the Mongols had started firing at the helicopters.

There wasn't any recent news footage available. Most of the content was just talking heads speculating on what was happening. The lack of information made the whole thing terrifying. As Dennis sat on his bed, listening to political commentators and military experts guess, on the condition of the island and the people, he wished he knew the truth. He'd rather have known for sure what was going on, whatever that horrible truth might be, than listen to the uninformed opinions of others. The reality had to be better than what he was imagining in his head.

"We have insider information that the taking of this small island is the first step in world domination for a new terrorist organization," one reporter said.

"This is what we've been warned about for decades, and it should be no surprise that it happened," said another journalist.

"The citizens of Verona could already be dead," a political commentator speculated. "The government is wasting time sitting around at Fort Lewis trying to decide what to do. Governor Serling is to blame here. This happened on his watch, and he's done nothing about it. What are they waiting for?"

Dennis turned off the TV, threw the remote on the bed, and walked with determination to Governor Serling's room. As he approached the door, he could hear the governor talking.

"But why would you want to put yourself at risk?" asked Governor Serling, trying to make a decision.

"Because Verona is all we have," Dennis responded from the doorway. He approached the table to join the conversation. "General, Governor . . . Verona is all Freddy, Mark, and I have. Our families are there, our jobs are there, our histories are there, and our futures are there. Our whole lives are there. And without Verona . . . I can't even think what would happen if we couldn't return."

Before the governor and the general could answer, Mark said to Dennis, "So, wait, you're not anti-LARP anymore?"

Dennis looked at Freddy, Jen, and Mark.

"Look, I really want to apologize for the things I said and did earlier. I was wrong. Yeah, there've been times when LARP has been the bane of my existence. But this whole invasion thing made me realize something . . . you can't live in the past, and the future isn't for sure. All we have is now. I've spent too much time wishing and thinking about how my life could have or should have been different. And it's been a waste of time. I am where I'm supposed to be."

Dennis faced the general and the governor.

"There's an old expression that says 'You can't go home again.' I don't believe it. I want to go home again, and I can, if you'll let me. Please, let us handle this. We want to fight for our home."

"How many people can you get together for this?" the general asked.

"About 200, maybe 225," Mark assured.

"Are you positive you can get that many people? I didn't think the Verona LARP faction was that big," the governor asked.

"It's not," said Mark, "but we can get everyone from our LARP league to join us."

"Would they do that?" the general asked.

"Are you kidding?" Dennis answered. "They would pay to do it! It would be a dream come true for them."

There were a few moments of silence before Governor Serling spoke again.

"I am going to call the president and tell him that I support your plan—"

"On one condition," the general jumped in, "if it goes badly, if I even think it's going badly, the US Army will be on standby to resolve the situation."

The governor nodded.

Shocked but trying to play it cool, Mark said, "Okay . . . well, we'll be in our room if you need us." As Mark, Jen, Dennis, and Freddy left the room, they could hear Governor Serling on the phone.

"Yes, this is Governor Serling of Washington State. I need to speak to the Commander-in-Chief, please."

"I can't believe that just happened," Jen said.

"Yeah, me neither," Freddy agreed.

"You just went and asked the governor if our stupid little LARP group can go and fight real live bad guys? And then he called the President to ask for permission?" Dennis said, as if repeating the scenario would help him believe it.

"Um, yeah," Mark said, still stunned that his plea had been effective.

The group entered their hotel room and sat on the beds. There were a lot of questions to answer in order to gather a LARP army in a short amount of time.

"How are we going to contact everyone to see if they'll do it?" Jen asked.

"And what if they say no?" Dennis said.

"How are we going to get real weapons?" Freddy added.

The questions weren't directed toward anyone specifically, they were just asked aloud, but the three expected Mark to take the lead in answering.

"Well, the first thing we gotta do is call Joe Peacock," Mark said. "He's still in Uniontown with everyone, and he can find out

[85]

how much support we can get. Once we know who's in, we'll call Larry to see if he can get us some battle gear. I'm sure he can."

"But what if we don't have any support from the rest of the LARPers?" Dennis asked, again.

"Well, at least we know that we tried," Mark answered.

"Do you really think this will work?" Freddy asked.

"It has to," Mark said. "Either that or the US Army goes in and wipes out Verona. So we have to try. Hey, how about calling Joe for me. He probably doesn't want to talk to me after what happened in Uniontown."

Freddy grabbed his cell phone and went out into the hallway to call Joe. It made him uneasy to see the towering military guard outside of the governor's room.

"Well, hopefully you can use all of your obnoxious LARPness for a higher purpose," Dennis said jokingly to Mark.

"Honestly, I'm really sorry about Uniontown . . . and everything else," Mark said, seriously. "This whole situation made me realize what's important and what isn't."

"Look," Dennis said, thoughtfully. "It's all in the past now. I never really hated you. Came close, though," Dennis said, trying to add some humor to the situation, "but the problem was more with me and less with you. I was focused on what I thought I'd lost because of all the time I've spent LARPing. I should have been thinking about everything I've gained from it. Some of the best times of my life have been spent running through the Outlook Woods with you, but sometimes I've been too focused on what was happening—or not happening—in other parts of my life, instead of the good that was happening. You know how it is, when you're mad at someone or something, all you remember is the bad stuff. So, I'm sorry, too—"

"If you two start hugging and kissing each other, I'm leaving," Jen said, trying to break the heaviness of the mood.

"Then why don't you come over here, sit on my lap, and stop me?" Mark said. She just rolled her eyes at him. The three of them looked at each other and laughed, surprised that they could make jokes under the circumstances.

Freddy entered the room and addressed the group.

"Just spoke to Joe. He's gonna talk to everyone, tell them what's going on and get back to me. Shouldn't take too long."

Over the next few hours, plans were discussed and laid out for the retaking of Verona. At the insistence of General Cassady, mostly to protect his daughter, the US Army would send fifty of its own troops to battle alongside the LARP group. Having the army as part of the invasion was also a condition made by the President, so they had no choice. The president was naturally worried about sending a group of untrained civilian warriors into a battle situation, but Governor Serling did an excellent job of convincing his commander-in-chief that a LARP army was really the most qualified army available.

The president had no idea what LARP was, but he warmed to the idea of the LARP army once it was explained. Of course, the media could know nothing about the retaking of Verona. That's the last thing that everyone needed. The invasion had to be a secret, as much as something could be a secret, in this age of instant electronic communication. They knew that the reporters at the Hulton Bridge covering the invasion certainly wouldn't keep the secret. And even though they were dedicated to living a medieval life, the Mongols certainly had knowledge of what a twenty-first century army could do.

This rogue army knew that the US would try to take back their land, but the army they expected wasn't the army they were going to get.

Mark got on the phone and called Larry, owner of Larry's World of Sports in Uniontown. It was a small store, with Larry as its only employee. Larry supplied weapon parts for the Hotzenbella kingdom, but could order just about any sport-related item, from a baseball bat to a mace. Mark liked Larry because Larry was a Vietnam War veteran who was very much into weapons and battle gear. Larry was also an armaments historian, and he often gave Mark historical background, and advice, for Hotzenbella purchases.

Larry was a closet conspiracy theorist who didn't trust the government, yet loved the country. He had a small arsenal in his home, and was ready for an invasion by a foreign power, which he thought he saw signs of in the news on a regular basis. He claimed to have met with past presidents, through business conferences, and always felt he had secret knowledge of the inner workings of the country. Larry was the perfect guy to supply the LARP army with real weapons for a real battle. Mark knew that he could trust Larry not to tell anyone of their plan to take Verona. Mark called Larry to get the battle plan in motion.

"Larry's World of Sports, Larry speaking."

"Larry, it's Mark."

"Mark, good to hear from you! I've been wondering if you were okay. How did you get off the island?"

"We were in Uniontown for the KNEL Fest when the invasion happened. Listen, I hate to cut you off, but we need weapons. Real ones."

Larry's voice lowered. "Okay . . . hold on. Let me get to a secure line. This line is being tapped." Mark heard two clicks, then Larry's voice. "Why do you need real weapons? What's going on?"

"Wait a minute, why is your line being tapped?"

"Because they know that I know what they're doing. My line has been tapped for years. That's why I got a secure line." Larry always thought he was under surveillance because of his knowledge and distrust of the government.

"But how do you know it's been tapped?"

"Because . . . I do. So what's going on?"

As Mark summarized the situation, Larry cut him off.

"So it finally happened."

"What?"

"The invasion of America. Don't you see? The Mongolians aren't Mongolians. They're part of the US Army!!!"

"What?"

"Mark, it all makes sense." Larry was talking faster, excited that, in his mind, one of his predictions had come true.

"This is the government's attempt at total control over its citizens. The 'Mongol' army . . . Mongols. Why would they pick Mongols? There's your hint right there that the whole thing's a cover-up. This 'Mongol' army is going to slowly creep onto the mainland and destroy the infrastructure there, too. It's all a part of the government's plan to take away our modern conveniences and control us."

"The President and the Army are backing us! They're even paying for the weapons! How can you say that?" Mark retorted.

"They're backing you because they want you to get slaughtered. They're sending you into a death trap!" Larry responded, passionately.

"Look, I don't have time for this. Can you get us the weapons we need or not?"

"Yes, 'cause here's what we're gonna do. I'm gonna arm your side so heavily that their 'Mongol' army—Mongols, what a bunch of amateurs—that they won't be able to beat you."

"Okay, good. Here's what we need—"

"I know what you need. Don't worry about it. Where do you want it sent?"

"Are you sure you know what to get? I mean, you don't even know how many people will be on our side. We don't even know how many people will be on our side."

"Don't worry, kid, I got this," Larry said, confidently. "I'll overnight it to wherever you need. Where do you want it?"

"Eiler's Hotel, Uniontown."

"Your arsenal will be there tomorrow afternoon. Gotta go, I've already said too much."

The phone clicked and there was a dial tone. Mark just shook his head and hung up.

The group continued to watch the TV news coverage in their hotel room at Fort Lewis. The helicopters that had been flying over Verona for the last few hours could no longer see the island, because of all the smoke rising from it. Reports confirmed that many buildings had been torched, and burned to the ground. From what the reporters could see before there was too much smoke, mountains of modern conveniences had been burned and destroyed, too. Computers, microwaves, refrigerators, ovens, washers, dryers, lamps—all of it was being burned in bonfires by the Mongols. Because no one could get to the island, speculative reports of civilian injuries, or deaths, flooded the airwaves.

The more the fires burned on Verona, the more the fire burned within Dennis, Mark, and Freddy to take the island back. They no longer felt helpless watching the news, because they had a plan. Yes, there were some holes in the plan, but they had a better idea of what to do than they did ten hours ago.

There wasn't hurt. There wasn't fear. There wasn't a longing. It was all determination to right this horrible wrong, and to save their home.

"Excuse me," said a large military policeman, who suddenly appeared in the doorway. "General Cassady would like to meet with all of you." The friends looked at each other, hoping that one of them knew what was going on. Had the President reconsidered? They turned the TV off, and headed next door.

They entered the room, and sat around the big, round table. Freddy was thinking that he had never seen a table that size, and of that sturdy quality, in a hotel room. Probably of oak or cherry wood. But this wasn't just any hotel room, and this wasn't just any situation.

"So, where are we in the planning for the retaking of Verona?" the general asked.

"Well, sir, I have secured weapons from a local supplier," Mark began.

"And I spoke to a friend of ours in Uniontown, who is covertly asking everyone there if they want to participate," Freddy added.

"Who is the weapons supplier?" the general asked.

Remembering Larry's paranoia, Mark kept his answer brief.

"He's a long time friend who has been supplying us with LARP weapon parts for years."

"Did you tell him what was going on?" the governor asked.

"Yes," Mark replied.

"Can you trust that he won't tell anyone else?"

"Yes, sir. Absolutely. He's a former military man. He understands these things," Mark said, trying to sound confident. He didn't believe Larry's conspiracy theory for a minute, but he didn't want Larry to be investigated by the government, either.

"Well, I've taken some steps to secure armament, too. I have issued a state mandate that all medieval weapons at the Seattle museum be removed and prepared for battle," Governor Serling said.

"We're gonna use real medieval weapons?" Mark said, excitedly.

"You're gonna use my weapons?" Jen said, her excitement much different than Mark's.

"To answer both of your questions, yes," the governor replied.

"You can't do that! That's my exhibit and that stuff is priceless!" Jen protested.

"Honey, for starters, those weapons don't belong to you, they belong to the museum. And the museum belongs to the state," the general responded. "The governor has the right to do whatever he sees fit with state property."

"Can't we just use the weapons we bought from Larry?" Jen pleaded.

"What if it's not enough? What if it's not durable or reliable?" the general countered. "Because of the craftsmanship of the museum's weapons, we know that they will be reliable. The museum has one of the largest medieval weapons collections in the country, and we have to utilize all of our resources. Like the governor said, the weapons are being prepared for battle as we speak."

Jen shook her head in disgust and said quietly to herself, "I can't believe you're doing this."

"Look, Jen," Dennis said, "I respect the history of those weapons almost as much as you do. But what we're doing here is bigger than the value of those weapons. Lives are at stake."

Jen nodded in sad agreement. "So how many Mongols are in Verona?"

"We don't know for sure," the general replied, "but, going by the news footage, we've seen three ships docked at the island, and we're figuring about 125 people per ship, so there's roughly 375 Mongols on the island. Now, that includes women and children, who probably won't be involved in the military conflict. Our estimate is that there's a Mongol army of 250-300 that needs to be removed from the island."

Just then, Freddy's cell phone rang. "It's Joe," he said, as he answered it. "Uh huh." Everyone in the room remained silent, trying to guess what Joe was saying. "Yeah, we're still doing it. Good. Well how many are there? Yeah, um, I don't know if they will accept that. Okay, I'll call you back." Freddy hung up the phone.

"He said that a majority of the LARPers in Uniontown is with us, but he doesn't have an exact number. When I asked him how many people he had ready to fight, he said 'a lot.'"

"Well, then how do we know what to plan for? He's got to give us a definitive number!" the general said, irritated. He was starting to wonder if this was such a good idea. Working with an amateur army that didn't even know how many were in its platoon didn't sound promising.

"I'm sorry, sir. I don't know what else to say," Freddy apologized.

"General," Dennis said, "I've known Joe Peacock forever. He's a good, honest guy. If he says there are a lot of people ready to go with us, then I believe him. I wouldn't be surprised if there were almost two hundred."

"I just don't like this," the general said. "You can't just go into a battle with 'a lot' of people. You can't base your training or supply on 'a lot' of people. As the ranking military officer in this state, I am, along with the governor, ultimately responsible for this mission. When the Commander-in-Chief asks me how many Americans are going to go and take back Verona, I can't just tell him 'a lot.' I mean, does your group really know what they're in for?"

"Honestly, General," Dennis spoke up, confidently, almost defiantly, "I really don't care what I'm 'in for.' All I know is that I can't go home right now, and I can't even call home right now, because a bunch of backward-thinking thugs won't let me. If I have to go over there myself, I will take that island back."

"And you gotta see it from our perspective," Mark joined in.

"LARPers really don't get any respect from people who know about us. LARPing is about as cool as collecting stamps or scrapbooking. This is the one big chance for a group of people, who have been put down since the first day they picked up a boffer, to actually do something with their hobby. A whole group of LARPers will finally get some sort of vindication in their lives."

The general studied their faces. They looked confident, and they looked ready. But, they had never seen war—real war—and he wondered if they would be able to fight in the face of it.

Freddy's phone rang again. It was Joe Peacock.

"Hey, Joe. Yeah, okay, that's great. I'll tell them. Oh, okay. Hold on. Governor, Joe Peacock would like to speak with you."

The governor, a bit puzzled, took Freddy's phone. "Hello?"

"Hello, sir. My name is Joe Peacock. I know that you are under a lot of stress right now, so I won't keep you. But I just want you to know that we have about 210 highly-trained warriors here ready to answer the call of freedom."

"Well . . . ah . . . thanks, Joe. We're doing what we can here to prepare."

"We await your orders, Governor."

Governor Serling, a slight smile on his face, gave the phone back to Freddy.

"We're ready when you are," Joe said. "We're not leaving Eiler's until we hear from you."

"Thanks, Joe. I'll talk to you soon." Freddy hung up.

"Two hundred ten," the governor said to General Cassady. "Plus our 50, that's 260. How's that sound?"

"Better," the general said, happy at the number, but still doubtful about the result.

"Well, I guess we better head to Uniontown then, huh?" Mark asked.

"Yeah, let's go to Uniontown," the governor said.

"I'm going with you to oversee this whole thing," the general said. "Be in the parking lot tomorrow at 0600. We'll leave then."

As Freddy, Mark, Dennis and Jen said their goodbyes, and

left the room, the general said "Jen, can I see you for a minute, please?"

Jen motioned for the others to go to their rooms.

"What's up?" Jen asked. But she knew what was coming.

"Sweetheart, listen. Although I am in agreement with the governor . . . mostly . . . I don't want you participating in this mission. It's not the place for you."

"Not the place for me?" Jen said, trying to control her indignation. She was used to the "daddy's little girl" stereotype, but didn't like it. "I guess the 'place for me' is right here at Ft. Lewis, right?"

General Cassady knew the ramifications of her tone, and tried to refine his message "Jen, those guys have something to fight for. Verona is their home. There's really no reason for you to go. You can just—"

"Stay here and be a woman?"

"Now, you know that's not what I mean."

"Then what do you mean?" Jen bristled.

Jen inherited her father's stubborn independence. Jack Cassady, father and general, was fighting with himself. "It's just . . . I don't want anything to happen to you. You're all I've got."

Jen softened, seeing her dad's concern. "I know Dad, I know. But I would never put myself in harm's way. I promise, if things are looking hairy, I'll get out of there."

Jack Cassady sighed, because he knew he couldn't stop her. Well, he could stop her. After all, he was in charge of this operation. But stopping her wouldn't benefit either of them. "Then do me a favor. Let me assign one of my personal guards to your unit. I want the best of the best there to watch over you."

"Okay, Dad," Jen said, hugging her father.

The general kissed the top of her head. "I used to kiss your head when you wore pigtails. Now you're going to wear a helmet."

"Dad, I'm not going to wear a helmet. It'll mess up my hair," Jen joked.

General Cassady shook his head at Jen's humor. "Go to bed, Jennifer Kathryn. You've got an early day tomorrow."

"Yes, sir, Daddy!" Jen replied, with a mock salute. General Cassady watched Jen enter her room, and then entered his, to continue planning with Governor Serling.

Governor Serling was at the table studying the map of Verona. General Cassady sat across from the governor, and pulled a wallet-sized photo from his decorated pocket.

"Ah, Ed, I've got something to show you," the general said. The next few minutes would be difficult, if they went the way the general expected.

"What's up," Ed answered, wearily, as he kept his head down, studying the map.

The general slid the picture a few feet in front of him, to the middle of the table. "Do you know this person?"

The governor removed his glasses, carefully placing them on the table. He picked up the picture, squinted. The photo was at least two decades old. In it, a young soldier looked intensely at the lens. His long nose made his lips appear thin, and his eyebrows were arched. The classic crew cut revealed a receding hairline.

"Yeah, that's Julian Wilkes," the governor finally replied. "I haven't seen him in twenty years, at least." The governor further studied the photo, as if he were reliving the memory. "Julian was a combative young man. A little too combative, sometimes. He trained under me at boot camp, right here at Fort Lewis." He looked at the general, waiting for an explanation as to why he had the picture from the governor's military past.

"Well, Ed, Julian is the head of this whole invasion thing," the general said, carefully.

The governor was confused. "So, we're not running the operation? Wait. Last I heard, Julian wasn't even in the service anymore."

"No, Ed. Julian is on their side," General Cassady replied.

Governor Serling sat back in his chair, in disbelief. "The Mongols?"

The general nodded.

"What's he doing with them?"

"We don't know," the general replied. "Our intelligence

regarding his involvement is sketchy at this point. The research shows that he attended the Stern School of Business at NYU, got a job at the stock exchange, and after that, he fell off the grid."

The governor shook his head, looking off in the distance. "I lost track of him after our stint here at Ft. Lewis. He seemed like an okay kid. Like I said, he seemed a little bit 'off' sometimes, but who doesn't at twenty? Why would a former military guy, who went to one of the top schools in the country, become a terrorist? He had every advantage this country has to offer. Something's missing here. Something doesn't add up."

"We'll continue to look into it, check out some more resources. But I just wanted to let you know that one of our own caused all of this."

The governor nodded, deep in thought.

Mark, Dennis, and Freddy were in their room, and Jen was in hers. Naturally, nobody slept.

Mark lay in bed, his stomach churning. This was unlike any LARP he had experienced. This time he would be a warrior for real. He lay in bed, eyes open, staring at the ceiling, making mental battle plans. But would the plans do him any good? While he realized what he had gotten into, he had no idea what was coming. He had never seen a real war before, never killed a man, or really even thought about it. And the Mongols certainly weren't going to have any rules in place. There was no back story here to follow, and if Mark told someone to lie down and die, they would keep coming. But what other choice was there?

To wait any longer would be crazy. If the group waited too long, there might not be anything left to fight for. And if the US Army went in, there wouldn't be anything left at all. Mark thought of his family, his non-LARP friends, his toy collection, and wondered if any of it was still there, and if it was there, was it the way he'd left it?

* * *

Freddy couldn't believe Mongolians were responsible for this. Of all the ethnicities in the world, why did it have to be his? Mongolians were mostly Buddhist. Weren't Buddhists supposed to be peaceful? Freddy thought of his family, and how proud they were of their heritage. How could he fight against his own people? But then he focused on the struggle, and triumph, of his family in achieving the American dream. They weren't rich or successful, but they were happy, and took advantage of the opportunity that America had given them. Above all, Freddy was loyal to his family. And his family needed him.

* * *

Dennis's mind wandered not to tomorrow, but to next week, next month, next year. The liberation of Verona had to be a rebirth for him. It had to. Things were getting too confining before he left for Uniontown. His relationship with Brad was almost non-existent, his friendship with Mark was vanishing, and his thoughts too often drifted to the past, and then to a future that would never be.

In a lot of ways, he was no different than Brad. Brad still loved to talk about his high school football heroics, and what might have been had he not gotten hurt playing ball. Dennis dwelled on the past he might have missed out on by spending too much time LARPing, and he spent too much time thinking about the future he lost because of LARP, and his friendship with Mark. He had to make peace with Brad, because Brad was the only family he had on the island since their parents had retired to Arizona a few years ago. Now, on the eve of the biggest day of his life, he was thinking about Brad. He worried Brad's warped view of himself could easily get him killed in the wrong situation. And the invasion was clearly the wrong situation.

As the Pacific wind howled outside, carrying with it the sounds of military vehicles coming in and out of the hotel parking lot, his thoughts were of Brad.

It was then that Dennis remembered Brad hadn't been alone

at the Rivertowne. Alyssa just had to show up for a visit during an invasion. He should have been there in Verona, with her, when it happened. If nothing else, he would have been there to protect her. Dennis knew he'd probably never see Alyssa again. If they ever got out of this situation alive, that is. She'd never return to Verona, and who could blame her? Maybe once he saw her, once this madness was over, he'd make one final attempt to connect with her. He could go back to Pittsburgh with her, and they could start a life together.

If Brad hadn't already put his slimy paws all over her.

If she wasn't traumatized by the invasion.

If she was still alive.

*   *   *

Freddy couldn't take it anymore. He could hear Mark and Dennis tossing and turning, so he knew that they were as awake as he was. He sat up in bed, began sorting through his bags, and got dressed.

"Hey, guys," Freddy said, somewhat quietly, "I'm gonna go take a walk. No point in layin' here and not sleeping."

"K, we'll be here," Mark said.

Freddy put his shoes on, and headed outside. He went down the long hallway, and turned right at the elevator bays. As he waited for the elevator, he noticed the military portraits lining the hallway. It was a who's who of American military history. Washington, Jackson, Grant, Eisenhower, Patton, and some others that Freddy didn't recognize, were looking very secure, and determined, this evening.

"Glad you look relaxed. Any advice for tomorrow?" he quietly asked the portrait of General Douglas MacArthur. The German proverb "no answer is an answer" went through his mind as MacArthur maintained his stoic silence. Freddy felt intimidated by their pictures. As a fellow soldier—for a short time, at least—he didn't want to tarnish their legacy.

A friendly "ding" sounded, and the elevator doors opened to reveal General Cassady. Because of the lateness of the hour, they were surprised to see each other. The general stepped out of the elevator.

"Hello, sir," Freddy said respectfully.

"Hello, Freddy. What are you doing up?"

Freddy didn't want to admit that he couldn't sleep, for fear of showing weakness to the general, but he had a feeling that the general already knew. "Just felt like going for a walk."

"Couldn't sleep, huh?" The general smiled warmly.

Freddy, embarrassed, answered, "No, sir."

"Anything you want to talk about?" the general asked. He sounded more like Jen's dad than a high-ranking US military man.

"Um . . ." Freddy started, comforted by the general's kindness, "I just . . . don't know what to expect tomorrow. I don't know what's going to happen, or not happen."

"Well, son, the unknown can always cause stress or fear, because we want to be in control of every situation at all times, but the best thing you can do is be prepared, not scared. Remember what FDR said: 'The only thing we have to fear, is fear itself.'"

"I know that you're right. Just wish I could go to sleep. I can never sleep when I know that something big is going to happen the next day. And seeing all the portraits of these famous military guys, and not being able to sleep 'cause I'm worried, makes me feel even more like I'm in the wrong place, at the wrong time, like there's no way I should be fighting under the same flag that they did."

The general smiled faintly. "We're in the same boat, soldier. Why do you think I'm still awake at this hour?"

"Really?" Freddy said.

"I've been at this for thirty years, and it never gets easier. Ever. I've looked at those portraits, too, hundreds of times. And you know what I see? Lots of tired men," the general said with a laugh.

Freddy, looking at the portrait of Eisenhower, said, "Ike does look kind of tired, doesn't he?"

"Of course he does," the general replied, reassuringly. "Trust

[99]

me, all these men were brave beyond the call of duty, but they were also human. They worried, they didn't sleep, and they questioned themselves. But they were always prepared, not scared. Now go take a quick walk and get to bed—0600 will come around a lot sooner than you think," the general said with a wink.

"Yes, sir," Freddy said, saluting then stepping into the elevator.

Freddy headed out of the lobby, and into the parking lot. He wanted to get his flashlight because the lot was dark, and he was worried about getting hit by a car. Getting injured in the parking lot would be the last thing he needed, especially the night before a battle that he already felt ill-equipped to handle. As he opened his car, and reached across the seat to the glove box, he heard the crackle of radio static. Freddy stopped for a moment, trying to think where it was coming from. As the crackle got louder, he turned the knobs on the car radio, but nothing happened. The car radio couldn't be on, anyway, because the car was turned off.

The crackle continued, and then he heard something else, something he'd heard his entire life and would recognize anywhere. His father's voice. Freddy immediately opened the back door of his car and began rifling through the clothes lying on the seat. He knew exactly what he was looking for—a black hand-held transistor radio. Freddy found the radio under an old blue sweatshirt that he kept in the car for chilly nights, and turned up the volume.

"If anybody can hear me, my name is Fred Urianhai, Sr., and I am on the island of Verona, off the coast of the state of Washington," Fred Sr. spoke in a slow, steady tone.

"The island has been taken by Mongols. I know that they are Mongols because I am of Mongolian descent. The Mongols have begun destroying the island . . . all modern conveniences are being destroyed."

Freddy hurriedly got his cell phone out of his pocket and called Dennis back in the hotel room. Freddy's heart rate increased with every ring of the phone. Dennis finally answered "What? I was just drifting off and you had—"

"Get out here . . . now. I'm in the parking lot in my car. Get dressed, get Mark, then run out here. And bring the general, too. Now, hurry!" Freddy hung up the phone so that he could listen to the radio. He didn't want to go into the hotel for fear of losing the reception.

Freddy's dad continued, "The Mongols are taking the citizens of Verona and locking them up in the bigger buildings in town. I'm locked in the Kiss plant with many other people. We've heard that others have been locked away at the high school, Riverview Park, and in the bank cellar. These areas are their strongholds."

Just then, Mark, Dennis, and the general came sprinting out of the hotel. As they got closer, Mark and Dennis heard the voice coming from the radio and immediately knew what was happening.

"Is he okay?" Mark asked, referring to Freddy's dad.

"He hasn't said."

"Is who okay? What's going on?" the general asked.

As Freddy continued to listen, Dennis explained, "Freddy's dad is a HAM radio operator. He has a battery-powered short-wave radio, and Freddy carries a transistor with him so that he can listen to his dad's broadcasts."

"And this man is on the island?" the general asked, intently.

"Yes, sir, he is," Dennis replied.

There was a deep silence as the men listened to the small radio. They were doing more than listening. It was as if the radio was feeding their starving souls.

"There's roughly 400 of them here, including women and children. Most of them are men ages 20-50. They don't have any modern weapons. No guns. Just swords, shields, axes, cannons. There haven't been any deaths that I know of, but there are injured people here. We tried to fight . . . but . . . we just couldn't. They came to our homes in big horse drawn carriages—they almost looked like small boats—and in their very crude form of English, told us to get into the carriages. They said that no one would be hurt, but when some of us tried to fight them, we were . . . punished. A neighbor of mine took a bat to one of them and all that got him was a shot to the head with a Morningstar, and a destroyed living room."

"I can't even believe this. I can't even believe this," Mark kept repeating.

"We think they sent scouts ahead of the invasion," Freddy's dad continued, "because there wasn't any confusion among them. They snatched us up and took us to designated areas. It was a very smooth operation on their part."

Another male voice was heard in the background. His comments were indecipherable, but Freddy's dad reacted immediately.

"What?" Then his voice got quieter. "My lookout says they're coming. If anyone is listening, please send help. They haven't killed anyone, yet, but anything could happen. I'll broadcast again . . . if possible . . . and, son, if you're out there, I . . ."

A hurricane of static returned. Freddy stood silent, motionless, hoping to hear the end of his father's sentence.

"Fred? Freddy?" Dennis said, quietly. Freddy was focused on the radio, but he finally looked up at Dennis. Tears of anger and fear filled Freddy's eyes. He was holding the small black radio with both hands, tightly, as if he would crush it.

"Let's go inside," the general said, cautiously. "We have to wake the governor and tell him about this."

"They can't do this . . . they . . . they just can't," Freddy said in astonished anger.

"I know they can't," the general said, "So let's stop them."

Freddy, looking like an angry, wounded animal, slowly turned and headed into the hotel. General Cassady, Mark, and Dennis followed.

"We need to get this going now, General," Freddy said firmly as they walked into the hotel, and headed down the hallway.

"I know," the general said evenly. Dennis, Mark, and Freddy could feel a shift coming from the general. He always felt that the situation was dire, but hearing Freddy's father on the radio sharpened the general's focus.

"That's my dad over there, General . . . my dad, just like you're Jen's dad," Freddy continued as the elevator took them to their floor.

"I know, Freddy, I know," the general responded again, in the same even tone.

They hastily walked to the governor's room. The general firmly knocked on the door.

"Governor?" he said in a gruff, military tone. The door opened almost immediately. Governor Serling was still wearing the same suit that he had worn earlier in the day. He didn't even bother to ask them to come in. He just turned away and headed toward the huge wooden table.

"New information has come to light, governor," said the general. "We have to act now."

While the general updated Governor Serling, Dennis studied Freddy. Freddy looked focused, intense, yet his mind was somewhere else.

"Okay, I'll call the Commander-In-Chief now and update him on the situation. You take care of things on your end," the governor said decisively.

The two men saluted each other, and everyone left the room, with the exception of Governor Serling who was dialing the White House.

"You guys get packed and ready," the general said. "I have a few things to do. Be in the parking lot in an hour."

Mark, Dennis, and Freddy headed to their room in silence. They were quiet as they packed. They were quiet as they exited the room, and they were quiet as they waited in the parking lot. Hearing Freddy's dad had made the situation real to them. Before, all they knew was what they saw on the news, and the whole thing still seemed like a nightmare that they would wake from at any minute. Retaking Verona was still an abstract concept. But now they had heard from someone that they knew and cared for, and it helped put a voice to the invasion.

Shortly after they got to the parking lot, they heard the rumble of trucks and saw a line of headlights heading toward them. The sight and sound was ominous, and if they weren't on a

US military base, they would have been scared. As the sun-like lights got closer, it was apparent that the vehicles were cargo trucks, ten of them. Dennis, Mark, and Freddy, in awe, watched the trucks park, their engines still humming, their lights still on. General Cassady appeared with Jen, and walked over to Dennis, Mark, and Freddy.

"Those ten cargo trucks are filled with one hundred of our best hand-to-hand combat troops. They're ready to go."

"I thought you said we were taking fifty troops with us?" Freddy asked.

"Well, things are a bit more . . . dire . . . than I had originally thought. We'll take one hundred, plus your group. The men I selected excel in hand-to-hand combat techniques. They are the best we have on this base. We need a swift and decisive victory."

The general's comment resonated with the group. It showed that he wasn't just dismissing the situation, and wasn't uninterested in their safety. It showed that they were going to work together, as opposed to working at the same time.

Freddy turned to the group. He was still focused on his dad's radio broadcast, and hearing it had changed his mood. The only thing that mattered to him right now was saving Verona, and nothing else.

"I'm not leaving for Uniontown with you."

"What do you mean? We need you there with us!" Mark asked, stunned.

"I want to tear those thugs apart, but I want to be smart about it. So I'm going to Verona. Right now," Freddy answered. His tone indicated that there was no changing his mind.

"But you'll get killed going there by yourself!" Dennis said.

"I'm not going there to fight. I'm going there to spy," Freddy said.

"What do you mean?" Dennis asked. The general just stood there, listening.

"My dad's broadcast gave us a rough idea of what's going on over there, but none of us have seen it for ourselves. Somebody has to go ahead to see how they're set up and get an idea of what we need to do. Since I'm Mongolian, I'll be inconspicuous. I'll put on my thief costume and I'll blend right in. They'll never notice."

"Well, the bridge is gone; how are you gonna get there?" Dennis asked.

"I know lots of people on the mainland who will loan me a boat."

Freddy knew that the general was quiet because he was taking the whole thing in, trying to judge whether or not this was a good idea.

"I know you're probably opposed to this, general, but it needs to be done. I'll try not to let anyone hear my accent, and they'll never know that I'm an American."

"I agree, Freddy. What can we do to help?" the general responded, to the amazement of the others.

"Daddy, we can't send him over there, by himself, with those barbarians!" Jen said, concerned.

"Honey, look, he's right. In order to protect our side, we need to know what's going on over there. He is the best one for the job."

Although Freddy appreciated Jen's concern, he didn't even address it. He needed to get to Verona quickly. "Here's my idea, General. Can you get a military boat?"

"I can get as many as you need," the general replied.

"Good. For now, I only need one. Here's the best way to do this: we'll have a military boat approach Verona, maybe fire some shots to get their attention. While that boat is keeping them busy, I'm going to go around the back of the island in my boat. There's some risk involved—"

"But there's risk in everything," the general said, finishing Freddy's thought. "Okay, head for Verona now. I'll call ahead to the military guard at the bridge and tell them you're coming, and what the plan is. I'll also have a military boat waiting for you at the bridge."

"Thank you, sir," Freddy said. He looked at Jen, Mark, and Dennis. They looked scared. Scared for Freddy, and scared that Freddy's plan officially signaled the start of the action. Nothing was said, but Freddy felt their concern and care.

[105]

"Okay, I'm going. Gotta get there to take advantage of the darkness. I'll see you back in Uniontown."

"You better," Dennis said.

"Don't worry. I wouldn't miss this for anything," Freddy assured.

Once everyone was packed, and the cargo trucks were ready to go, everyone headed to their cars. As Dennis started his car, there was a knock on the passenger side window. Mark, who was sitting in the passenger seat, looked to see who was knocking, then turned to Dennis with a stunned look on his face.

"Roll the window down. Who is it?" Dennis said.

Mark rolled the window down. It was Governor Serling. "Got room for one more?"

"Uh, yeah, sure," Dennis said, confused.

"You're coming with us?" Mark asked.

"Yep," the governor said, as he opened the back door of the car.

"To Verona?" Mark asked, again.

"Yep," Governor Serling said again.

"Why?" Mark asked, in disbelief.

"Well, Mark, it turns out that the person leading the Mongols is someone I used to know. I want to go over there to see if I can bring him back alive."

"So you're going to Verona with us?" Dennis asked.

"You bet," the governor said, confidently.

"I'm sorry, Governor, we're just . . ." Dennis said. He wanted to say "surprised", but didn't want to insult the governor.

"I know, but don't be. I told you, I LARPed for years before I got into politics. I can sling a sword with the best of 'em. And don't forget, I served as a paratrooper in the 511th Parachute Infantry Regiment of the 11th Airborne Division. Invasions are my thing."

"I didn't know that, Governor," Dennis said, happily surprised.

"Don't worry about it. And by the way, we're all soldiers now . . . call me Ed."

"Cool!" Mark said with a smile.

"Call Joe Peacock," Dennis directed Mark. "Tell him we're on our way and to be in the parking lot with everyone by dawn."

Dennis's car headed for the exit of the Fort Lewis Hotel. They were going north on Route 5 to Uniontown. Jen and the general followed in Jen's car, and behind them rumbled ten, well-lit, soldier-carrying US Army cargo trucks. .

CHAPTER 12

The drive from Fort Lewis to Uniontown was unusually fast. Dennis drove with determination, taking out his frustration on the road. The hum of his engine became his heartbeat, and the car a part of him. It was as if he were pushing the car harder, faster, willing it to get to Uniontown instantly, so that this nightmare could end. He figured that no state trooper would stop him with an army convoy behind him.

And if he were stopped, the governor was in the back seat.

Although sleep hadn't been a priority in the last twenty-four hours, there were no signs of weariness. The group was driven by the indignity of the invasion of their home, and by the thrill of taking action. There was no more waiting to be done. Soon, they would be back on Verona, and in Verona, and they would be very different than when they'd left. The island would be different, too.

They were also driven by the unknown. What was going on in Verona and how bad was it? Hopefully, Freddy would have some answers.

If he returned.

The sun began its slow ascent into the clear blue sky as the convoy neared Eiler's Hotel in Uniontown. Mark was the first to notice the parking lot, as Dennis was solely focused on what was directly in front of him.

"What is that?" Mark asked.

"What?" Dennis asked.

Mark took his glasses off and cleaned them as Ed leaned forward. "I see something, too," he said.

Mark put his glasses back on, but still couldn't make out what was happening. He reached in the back seat of the car, where Dennis had his telescope. Lowering the window, he put the telescope to his eye and smiled. "Sweet," he said.

"What?" Dennis asked again, getting a bit impatient.

"Looks like they're ready. I'm surprised they all showed. You know how flaky LARPers can be," Mark said, still smiling as he handed the telescope to Ed, who took his turn looking through it.

Within moments, the convoy entered Eiler's parking lot. The lot was filled with LARPers, in full regalia, waving their weaponry in the air as a greeting. The sun ricocheted off of each piece of faux metal, duct tape, and fiberglass, giving the LARPers an otherworldly glow. The flags from each kingdom proudly waved, welcoming their fellow warriors. A broad smile sneaked across Dennis's face, and Ed laughed in the back seat.

As Dennis parked his car, Joe Peacock walked up to him.

"How's that for a greeting?"

"Incredible!" Dennis said, feeling a sense of pride in his fellow LARPers. Mark and Ed got out of the car, and Dennis introduced Ed to Joe.

"Joe, this is Ed."

"Hi. Wow, you look a lot like the governor," Joe said, laughing.

Dennis stepped in. "Ah, Joe, this is the governor."

Joe stopped laughing and arched his eyebrows. "Huh?"

"Nice to meet you, Joe. Yes, I am the governor, but until this conflict is over, I'm Ed. I'm a former, and current, I guess, LARPer with a military background. And I'm fighting this battle with you."

Joe turned to Dennis.

"When this is over, you gotta tell me the whole story about what happened at Fort Lewis."

Dennis smiled. "Will do. Did Larry send the weapons?"

Joe pointed to several huge wooden crates across the parking lot. "Yep." The crates had FRAGILE spray-painted on each side, and the boards were bowing under the weight and girth of the contents.

"Did any arrive from the Seattle Museum?" Ed asked Joe.

"Yes, sir . . . um . . . Ed. They're over there with Larry's stuff. Looks like you brought some backup," Joe said, motioning toward the cargo trucks where troops and gear were unloading.

"Yeah, the general really stepped up. We've got 100 hand-to-hand combat experts ready to go," Dennis answered.

The general approached Joe, Mark, Ed, and Dennis. "Dennis, round up all the kings and have them meet me in the conference room in thirty minutes. It's time to start planning."

Joe turned immediately, and began rounding up his fellow kings.

The employees and other patrons knew something was going on. The number of military personnel and presence of cargo trucks made it kind of obvious, but, for all they knew, the US military was planning something, and was using Uniontown as a temporary meeting place. They had no idea that the LARPers they saw every year, the same ones who got drunk in the bar, and chased each other around the hallways, screaming and wielding swords, were planning to retake Verona.

The kings of the five kingdoms involved in the LARP league, plus Joe Peacock, met with General Cassady and Governor Serling in the conference room. The room was hardly ever used. It only existed so the Eiler family could advertise "the convenience of our luxury conference room." The luxury included a white board and a projector.

The LARP kings were Steve Alessi of South Hills, Bob Palermo of Penn Hills, Emily Stokes of Beaumont (the only female to have her own kingdom), Bob Schwartzmeier of Castle Shannon, and Anthony Masi of Brooklyn Park. Their kingdoms were on the mainland of Washington State. All of the kings had been LARPers for years. The two Bobs were senior members of the league, having been involved for over three decades. Although the competition was fierce during league battles, there was no bad blood among the kings, and everyone was happy to work together to retake Verona.

The small conference room buzzed with questions, but everyone settled down and took their seats as Governor Serling closed the door and General Cassady stood up to speak.

"Ladies and gentlemen, my name is General Jack Cassady. My daughter, Jen, is a member of your LARP league in the Verona army. I am the ranking military officer in the state, and

I'm headquartered at Fort Lewis on the mainland. As you are well aware, from the news coverage, the island of Verona has been invaded. The invaders are a rogue group from Mongolia who left their country because they despise the twenty-first century advancements there and want to turn Verona into a medieval colony. Our intelligence also confirms that the rogue Mongols want to use Verona as an outpost-for-rent to America's enemies so that they can plan attacks on our soil. We can confirm that this group has their own leader who organized the Verona invasion. While the US military is confident in its ability to retake Verona, we fear that the overwhelming force would result in too many civilian casualties on the small island and have therefore decided, at the suggestion of the Verona LARP faction, to retake Verona using a mix of your LARP league and US military personnel skilled in hand-to-hand combat. Our objective over the next twenty-four to thirty-six hours is to train this new army to retake Verona. While I understand that all of you are skilled in medieval warfare, it is important that we become accustomed to each other and the weapons we will be carrying. The purpose of this meeting is to give you relevant information to pass on to those in your kingdom. Are there any questions?"

"So it's all true, huh?" Steve asked.

"Yes, I'm afraid it is," the general responded.

"What exactly will be required of us?" Bob Schwartzmeier asked. "I mean, are we going to have to . . . kill them? I'm just . . . . a retired teacher who works at a golf driving range. The only things I've ever killed are the chipmunks who don't get out of the way of the range vac . . ."

"Our goal is to keep causalities to a minimum, sir," the general answered. "However, some situations may call for . . . specific actions that are out of the realm of your day-to-day activities."

"So we're gonna have to kill people, then?" Emily asked.

The general didn't want this meeting to turn into a seminar about the various ways to kill the enemy. He didn't want the kings to walk out before the training had even begun. In the back

[111]

of his mind, the general worried that, once the reality of what lay ahead came to light, these civilians, who never handled a real weapon, would back out. Then he would have to take care of it in a way that he didn't want to think about.

"Let me assure all of you," the general said, "we don't want you to go in there thinking that you have to slaughter the Mongols, and we don't want you going in there thinking that you are going to get slaughtered. We have two plans in place to make sure that neither scenario happens. First, if things look ugly, if they even smell ugly, you are ordered to bail out immediately and head back to the mainland. Second, we are going to surround the island with landing craft, so that the Mongols can be captured and moved onto the ships. Our goal is not to kill them, but to capture them. Intelligence is being gathered to ensure the success of our plan."

Bob Palermo spoke up. "And where is this intelligence coming from? I thought no one could get to the island?"

Governor Serling answered, "One of your own, Freddy from Verona, has volunteered to go to the island to gather intelligence on the condition of the island and the positioning of the enemy. He's there as we speak."

"Freddy's Mongolian, isn't he? How do we know he's not one of them? He coulda set the whole thing up," Anthony asked.

Recalling the image of Freddy listening to his dad's radio broadcast, the general answered, sternly, "Freddy is not one of them."

There was silence as the tension in the room grew.

The governor spoke up. "I'm sorry, I didn't introduce myself. As you may know, my name is Ed Serling, and I am the governor of the state of Washington. I have spoken to the Commander-in-Chief, and he is aware, and approves of, our plan. I am a former LARPer with a military background, and I will be fighting right alongside you."

"Wow. You're really going over there with us?" Emily asked.

"Yes, I am."

"'Bout time a politician worked for his money," Anthony

said, and everyone laughed.

"Now look," the general said, getting back to business. "I want to be clear . . . we do not expect you to go over there with the intent of killing everyone. Your goal is to capture and lead them to our landing craft." The general paused before saying the next part because he knew the answer would make or break the mission.

"If any of you . . . if any of you have any doubts about your ability, or the ability of your army, to effectively participate in this mission . . . then please tell us now."

Bob Schwartzmeier raised his hand.

"Um, General Cassady"

"Yes?"

"Uh, if we retake Verona, we will get to meet the president?"

The general smiled. "I'm sure that can be arranged."

The six kings looked at each other, and nodded.

"Okay, we're in," Steve said.

The general was happily surprised. He had one last question. "Just out of curiosity, why are you risking your lives for Verona?"

"Well, for me," Bob Palermo said, "it's like this, we're helping our LARP friends from Verona. And who's to say these Mongols aren't going to want to come to the mainland and take over my town? Penn Hills isn't too far from Verona. We gotta stop them now."

"Yeah, and the other thing is," Joe Peacock added, "we talked about this before you guys showed up—the other thing is that we all wanna see how we'd do fighting a real war with the skills we have. We've been practicing this stuff for years against each other. It's kinda like how every college football player wonders how he'd do with the pros, you know?"

"But let's be clear about this," the general said. "This isn't a game."

"Well, no, but it's the same idea," Joe said. "Find 'em, pummel 'em, drag them to the end zone, which, in this case, is the boat."

"Okay, then," the general said, pleased that everyone was

supportive of the plan. "The next thing I need you to do is to gather your armies and tell them what we have discussed here. Open the weapons crates in the parking lot and go through whatever training exercises you normally do. You're really going to have to put some time in, because the real weapons are probably heavier than the ones you normally use. Also, I expect that you will share your training with the men from Fort Lewis, and I expect that you will learn hand-to-hand combat strategies from them. We all have to work together to get this over with as quickly and efficiently as possible. I'll meet you and your armies in the hotel restaurant at dusk. Bring your appetites, 'cause tonight's on Uncle Sam." .

CHAPTER 13

Freddy arrived at the Hulton Bridge just as the last bit of blackness of night was fading. He parked his car at a nearby gas station, quickly changed to his LARP costume, and, heart racing, jogged down Hulton Road, toward the bridge. He could smell the smoke from the fires burning on the island, and the darkness coming from Verona was greater than any light he had ever seen. Freddy had driven up and down Hulton Road thousands of times in his life, but it felt, and looked, so very different that, if he didn't know where he was, he wouldn't have recognized it.

A kaleidoscope of emotions was flashing though his consciousness—fear, sadness, anger. Regardless, he had to do what he set out to do, because no one else could do it. Who would have ever thought that being Mongolian in Washington State would be something that could help save the country?

Okay, maybe not the whole country, but part of it.

Freddy's breathing grew shallow as he approached the military police at the bridge. He walked up to the nearest officer and said, "Hello, I'm—"

Before he could say his name, the MP grabbed him by the throat, and slammed him stomach first onto the ground. Freddy could feel the MP's knee on his neck

"Where do you think you're going?" the MP growled.

"Wait, no, I'm not—" Freddy tried to answer, as he tasted his own blood coming from his lip.

"Shut up!" the MP barked in his ear. He then hollered over to another group across the street "Sarge? I think I got one here . . ."

Within seconds, Freddy was surrounded by more MPs, and he could hear guns being cocked. He saw a pair of black boots, and heard the voice belonging to the boots say, "At ease."

The man crouched down, and menacingly said in Freddy's ear.

"Just who in the hell do you think you are, trying to cross my bridge? You people have done enough damage to that bridge. If you want to go across so bad, maybe we oughta take you out there and hang you from it."

Freddy could feel his body filling with superhuman strength. He felt he could take them all on, obliterate their whole beings, and make them feel pain that they couldn't even comprehend.

If only he could get up.

Freddy spoke with as much menace as he could.

"My name is Freddy Urianhai. I was sent here by General Cassady from Fort Lewis."

The Sergeant immediately got on his two-way radio and said, "He's here." Then addressing the MP who still had his knee in Freddy's back, "Let him up."

"But Sarge . . ." the MP protested.

"He's not one of them. Let him up," the Sergeant commanded.

The MP helped Freddy up and dusted him off. "I'm Sergeant Morrison. I'm sorry. It's just that—"

"I look like one of them, I know," Freddy said, indignantly, as he cleaned himself off.

Sergeant Morrison, fearing that the incident would be reported to General Cassady, said, "Is there anything I can do for you? Can I have the medic look at your lip?"

"No," Freddy said. "I just want to get to the island. Where's my team?"

"They're at the dock, waiting for you," Sergeant Morrison said. Freddy focused his eyes ahead, as he walked away.

As he navigated the small hill that led down to the dock, he licked his lower lip, the warm, metallic taste still there. He wondered if his friends and loved ones on the island tasted their own blood, too. A brief tussle with the MP was a small price to pay for the freedom of the Verona.

Freddy saw the landing craft parked at the dock. Morning was fast approaching, and Freddy knew he had to leave immediately if he was going to have a fair chance at landing on the island unnoticed. There were five soldiers standing on the deck of the craft. A few of them were testing the giant floodlight; another was loading the on-board weaponry; and there was an additional soldier looking at the island through military-grade binoculars.

Freddy, in no mood for small talk, approached the boat. "I'm Freddy Urianhai. I've been sent here by General Cassady. Are you ready to go?"

The soldier with the binoculars turned to Freddy. "Yes, we're ready. What's the plan?"

"I need you to get their attention while I go around to the far side of the island and dock."

"Do you have a boat?" the soldier asked.

"Yeah, there's a boat at the next dock over that I have the keys to. It belongs to a friend."

"Okay," the soldier replied. "We're going to use our loudspeakers to get their attention. We'll say something about wanting to negotiate, and I'm sure they'll fire on us, like they did on the Red Cross. At that point, we'll fire back, but nothing heavy. Just enough to keep them engaged. How much time will you need to get to the island safely?"

"About twenty minutes," Freddy said. It would probably take him ten, but it was better to have too much time than not enough.

"All right. Let's get to it. Start heading for the island."

Freddy nodded and walked over to the boat at the next dock. The keys were hidden under one of the seats, and Freddy found them easily. Freddy fired up the boat, and the hum of the craft's engine reminded him of all the times he had used the boat on fishing trips with his dad.

"I'm coming, Dad," he whispered. He accelerated the boat slowly and smoothly, so as not to draw attention to himself. He didn't want to make waves, literally and figuratively. He looked over his left shoulder, and could see the landing craft heading directly to the island. Freddy let them get ahead of him, even though in his heart he wanted to step on the throttle and go as fast as possible to the island. But this was a waiting game, and he wasn't going to let an impulsive act cost him a victory.

He heard the megawatt loudspeaker from the landing craft.

"Attention Mongols occupying the island of Verona. This is the United States Army. We want to negotiate the release of the civilians on the island."

Almost immediately, there was a thunderous boom. The Mongols must have been watching for them to fire that quickly. Had they seen Freddy head toward the island, too? The landing craft continued to head toward the island, cautiously. The soldiers aimed their huge floodlight at the cannon. It looked like the sun itself was beaming from the boat.

"We are not here to fight. We just want freedom for the United States citizens of Verona," shouted the officer.

Another cannon shot fired at the boat. Freddy accelerated his boat, knowing that it wouldn't be heard above the cannon shots and loudspeaker. The island was easily in view, but he didn't want to go too fast and draw attention to himself. Freddy heard the repeated shots of what sounded like a machine gun, no doubt from the landing craft. More cannon shots followed the gunshots. The more noise and commotion Freddy heard, the faster he went.

Approaching the island, he veered to the right, going in a horseshoe direction to the back of the island to dock. There wasn't an official dock there, so he'd have to just park in the sand of the beach. His heart rate accelerated, as he felt the sand of the Verona beach slow up the boat, until he finally came to a stop. He quickly walked to the end of the boat and jumped off, landing on the beach.

Freddy was standing on Verona.

He was home. Deep down, he wanted to stop and relish the moment, but the clock was ticking. The chaos between the landing craft and the Mongols roared in the dawn.

Freddy took off running, taking advantage of the noise, and the sweet distraction that would allow him to see for himself what had happened to his beloved home, and, more importantly, his dad.

Freddy ran harder than he had in a very long time. He ran with purpose, up the beach and into the nearest patch of woods.

Luckily, Verona was mostly surrounded by woods, so it wasn't too hard to find a place in which to catch his breath. He knew each part of the forest well, from all the years he spent LARPing in them. Freddy smiled as he realized that the LARPers had a huge advantage. They knew the island, every inch of it. To the Mongols, Verona was a foreign jungle.

Freddy moved though the woods like a wolf on a hunt. While he would scout the island as best he could, he would also head for the Kiss plant. He had to find his dad. Plus, if what his dad said was accurate, the Mongols were camped out around the Kiss plant, so it was a lucky coincidence that his personal mission coincided with his official mission. Anyone else would do the same thing.

He made his way to the woods behind the Kiss factory. It didn't take him long to get to the hill that backed the factory. To get to the rear entrance, he'd need to safely navigate a hundred-foot drop to the parking lot. Freddy slowly began his descent, cautiously moving down the hill. The last thing he needed was to slip and roll all the way down. If he got hurt, the whole mission would be compromised. The team would have no idea what was going on in Verona because Freddy would never be able to return.

That, and he'd probably be discovered, and killed, by the Mongols.

Freddy made it safely down the hill to the Kiss parking lot. He wanted so badly to look around, and he would look around, but, first, he had to get into that plant and find his dad. Freddy dashed for the back door. As he quietly jiggled the handle, he thought of his grandparents. They tried so many times to teach him their native language, and the history of the language, and just to appease them, he feigned interest.

"Someday, you'll want to know this," his grandma would tell him when it became clear that he wasn't paying attention. Grandma must have been a prophet, because right about now he wished he had paid attention. If he got caught, or even spotted, he would have to somehow work his way out of the situation, and knowing the language would have been a big help. He knew a few words in Mongolian, but if the conversation went past exchanging pleasantries or finding out where the nearest bathroom was, he was done.

The door was locked, as were the next few back doors that he came across. He didn't want to rattle the doors too hard, but at the same time, he couldn't just knock on the front door and ask to see his dad.

Freddy looked around, and took a few steps back. As he studied the surface of the building, he saw several opened windows, about fifteen feet up, preceded by a small landing. The windows were kept open year round, to let all the heat out of the plant. He anxiously opened the green pouch slung over his shoulder, and pulled out a bull rope with a hook at the end. Freddy twirled it, and tossed it up to the landing in front of the window. There was a clanking noise, and the rope and hook came right back at him, narrowly missing his head.

He waited a minute, to see if the miss drew any attention. Freddy held his breath, so that he could better hear if there was someone coming. All he heard was his heartbeat.

Again, he twirled the rope, tossed it up . . . and crash. Freddy had overshot and busted the window. He wasn't going to wait to see if anyone came this time.

He had to either get on the roof or run back into the woods.

Freddy yanked on the rope, and, gritting his teeth, twirled it again, shooting it up to the roof.

Clank.

The rope didn't come back at him. He tugged on it with all of his weight. When it didn't budge, Freddy quickly scampered up the wall to the landing, right before the window. Pulling the rope up, he threw himself down flat, level with the wall. The silence endured; no one was talking, and no one was coming. Freddy smelled the sweetness of the Kiss beverages emanating from the window. The smell had been a part of his surroundings his entire life, and it smelled sweeter than ever.

Freddy peered through the broken glass. The plant floor was empty, except for the machines. There were bottling machines, labeling machines, capping machines, and filling machines, but all of them sat silent, probably for the first time in decades. The huge brewing silos looked the same as always. Each one was a different color; purple, red, orange, and green, representing the flavors that were brewed in each.

Freddy surveyed the floor for a few seconds. He didn't see anyone, and didn't hear any movement. The Mongols were so careless with security. For all the time they spent invading the island and rounding up the citizens, they weren't doing anything to make sure that no one escaped.

Or got in.

Strangely enough, he couldn't hear the voices of the Veronaites, either. They had to be in a storage room somewhere. The Kiss factory was a popular grade school field trip destination, and Freddy had toured it several times. The plant was big, but Freddy knew the layout, and there were only a few storage rooms. The Kiss drinks were shipped so quickly that there really wasn't a reason to store them in the factory. He looked over the factory floor and planned out his route to each storage room. He had to visit each one, quickly, and get out as fast as possible.

Freddy quietly landed on the floor, and opened the nearest door. A roomful of people jumped back in terror. Some of them were wearing their Kiss work clothes, others were wearing pajamas. They all looked weary, and frightened. Freddy closed the doors behind him, and scanned the group, looking for a familiar face. He saw one; his eighth grade teacher, Mary Chirdon. She had been his favorite teacher, and they still kept in touch. He quickly walked up to her, as others in the room gasped. Mary cowered as Freddy approached. Quickly looking over his shoulder, Freddy removed his hood.

"Mrs. Chirdon, it's me. It's Freddy," he said to her, calmly, yet urgently.

She studied his face for a moment and, realizing that it was him, said, "Freddy . . . what are you doing here?"

"I don't have a lot of time," he said, quietly, "But help is on the way. Are you okay?" He turned to face the rest of the group. "Is everyone here okay?"

The group, realizing that he was one of their own, relaxed and nodded.

"My dad is Fred Urianhai who works at the Rivertowne. I know that he's here somewhere. Has anyone seen him? Does anyone know where he is?"

A man spoke up. "Yeah, I saw him. He's here. He's gotta be in one of the storage rooms. They put all of us in storage rooms."

A woman asked, "What do you mean, 'help is on the way'? Who's coming? The army?"

"Yeah, sort of. Trust me, this will all be over soon. I just need all of you to be strong . . . and be ready. We're going to need you."

Freddy turned to Mrs. Chirdon again. "Be strong, it's almost over." Freddy told the group, "Don't tell anyone I was here." Then he put his hood on and headed to the next storage room.

The second room was right next to the first. As soon as Freddy opened the door, he felt a blow to his cheek and a kick to his stomach. He was on the floor instantly, being kicked and hit.

"This ends now!" a voice said. Another voice joined in. "We're takin' the island back, starting with you!"

"Wait, stop, I'm not one of them. I'm one of you! Stop! Stop!" Freddy choked out.

The kicking continued.

Didn't they hear him? Didn't they recognize him? The island was so small, everyone knew everyone else; they had to know. He tried to remove his hood so that they could see his face.

"Stop, I'm with you!"

A voice from the back of the room yelled, "Freddy? Son?" Suddenly, Freddy felt another body on top of his, protecting him. "This is my son, this is my son, stop!!!" Freddy's dad said to the angry crowd. The kicking and punching stopped, and everyone backed away.

Apologies could be heard, and one man said, "I'm so sorry, Fred. It's just that—" Freddy's dad gave the man an angry look before he could finish his sentence. Fred Urianhai Sr. had a strong physical presence, and an intense stare that could stop a rabid dog—a trait he had passed on to his son.

Freddy's dad got off of him, and helped him sit up.

"Son, what are you doing here? You have to get out. You could get killed here."

Coughing and shaking, Freddy said, "I don't have the time to go into detail, but help is coming. I need all of you to stay strong, and be ready. I'm coming back with help, lots of it, and we'll need all of you to help us retake the island."

Freddy looked at his dad. Their eyes met. He looked tired, older than he had just a few short days ago.

"C'mon, Dad, let's go. We can be outta here and off the island in twenty minutes."

"Son, I can't," he said, quietly.

"What do you mean that you can't? You have to!" Freddy protested.

"Freddy, I can't. I have to stay here with the rest of the town. I can't leave."

"Why not?" Freddy was getting angry. "They'd leave you in a minute. Didn't you see what they just did to me?"

"That was a misunderstanding. I can't leave now. Once we separate, once we show weakness, they've won. We have to stick together."

The anger that had been bottled up inside of Freddy was now too great to control. He stood up, grabbed his dad by the arm, as if his father were a misbehaving toddler, and said, "Let's go! You're coming with me!"

His dad gently pulled his arm away. "Freddy, I'm staying. If for no other reason, I have to stay here and broadcast."

"Who cares about the broadcast? It doesn't matter anymore because we're coming back to free everyone."

"Freddy, it does matter. Things can change so fast here, and the broadcasts will keep everyone informed. I appreciate you coming here, but you need to go and do what you have to do. Please, we'll be fine."

Freddy fought to hold back tears of anger and pain. It was clear that his dad wasn't coming. And he knew he needed to leave, so that he could brief General Cassady.

"I'll be waiting here for you, son. We all will."

Freddy embraced his father. He didn't want to let go, but he had to. If he wanted to save the group, he had to let go. He kissed his dad on the cheek and headed out. Going straight to the window, Freddy climbed the rope and was on the roof in a few short seconds. He quickly rappelled down the back side of the building to the parking lot, and went back into the woods.

Freddy dashed through the trees. He felt himself smiling, as warm tears trickled down his scraped cheek. As badly as Freddy wanted his dad right next to him, he was proud that Fred Sr. stayed with the group. Father and son were stubborn, proud, and loyal, sometimes all at once. Freddy could feel his father in him, with him, as he cut through the forest.

The dense woods would serve as his cover. Freddy could get to most any part of the island through the woods, and easily sneak back in if things got tight. He would use the woods to get to Verona High School.

As he made his way to the high school, Freddy thought of all the LARP battles he had fought in the woods. He had so many incredible memories attached to this area. He had personal memories of certain trees, a bend in the creek, and an oddly-shaped bush. Just over the small hill somewhere was a particular thin tree, among many, where, as high school freshmen, he, Mark and Dennis had carved their initials—MFD—in the bark. As Freddy passed the small hill, he wondered if the tree had lasted as long as their friendship.

A little farther up the trail Freddy saw the bush that was in the shape of a donut. The bush was tilted at a forty-five degree angle, and part of the middle of the bush had died, so it was hollow. It was there, during one of their first LARP battles, that Mark had jumped out of the hole to surprise the enemy with a paralyzing spell, only to find that, as he leaped out, his cape got stuck on a branch and his whole costume tore off from the back. Mark, as usual, stayed in character, but his opponents didn't, falling to the ground in hysterics at the sight of Mark's Dungeons & Dragons boxer shorts. Freddy wanted to stay and visit those memorials (what if he never saw them again?) but he had to keep on. He was making good time, and he had to keep moving.

Freddy peeked out of the woods at the road leading to Verona High. It was clear, as far as he could see. He could easily enter the school through the back, as he had at the Kiss plant. But if he did, he wouldn't be able to see the status of the entire building.

To see everything, he would need to take the short road that led to the school's front entrance. All he had to do was walk a few short blocks, enter the school, look around, and leave as quickly as he came. He pulled his hood over his head, put his chin to his chest, so as not to draw attention to himself, and headed to the school. Freddy had to walk confidently, like he belonged there. He did belong there! This was the school that he, Mark, and Dennis had graduated from. But, as of right now, it belonged to these rogue Mongolians, and he had to play the part.

The road was L-shaped, and as Freddy headed down the long stretch, he could see a troop of Mongolian guards posted at the turn, out of the corner of his eye. He slowed his pace a-half-a-step, not enough to be noticed, but enough to give him a few precious seconds to come up with a plan. Should he turn and run? He'd probably be chased if that happened.

Should he forget about going into the school, just keep walking down the road and hide in the woods awhile to see if the guards went away? No, there wasn't enough time for that.

He nervously decided to stick with his original plan and head to the school. Freddy had to walk confidently toward the gate and up the road to Verona High. He wouldn't look at the guards, but he wouldn't look away, either. As he got closer, he tried to walk calmly.

The guards, three in all, were standing to the left of the entrance. Freddy headed in, walking to the middle right of the narrow road. He didn't want to walk on their side, but he didn't want to stick to the right side, either. That would make it look like he was avoiding them.

The guards were dressed in medieval attire, just like the reports suggested. They wore metal helmets, with a long, sharp point at the top. The helmets covered their ears, and had protective flaps in the back. Two red feathers decorated each side. They wore armor, but it wasn't metallic, it was some sort of thick animal skin. The armor was fashioned to look like the gills of a fish and went down past their knees. They wore arm bracers, too, similar to their body armor. All three guards had facial hair, either beards or long goatees.

The guards were talking in Mongolian as Freddy passed. He walked up the road as if he were one of them and passed the guards without incident.

Or so he thought.

Freddy was about fifteen feet away from the guards when one of them called out to him. He walked a few more steps, then turned around. The guards signaled for him to approach them. His mind raced, and he thought he felt his heart stop beating for a minute. If he was ever going to run, now was the time.

His dad, and Verona, needed his bravery, not impulsive cowardice. Freddy had to continue for the good of the mission.

Freddy slowly looked up from his hood. He didn't want to look at them directly, for fear they would see his blended American heritage. The last few hours really made Freddy feel like an outcast because of his appearance. His fellow Americans had beat him, twice, for looking Mongolian. And now, his native people could very well kill him for being American.

A guard spoke to Freddy in Mongolian. "Where are you going?"

Freddy knew that phrase well, because his grandparents had asked him that all the time as a child.

Freddy pointed to the school and replied in Mongolian, "To the school." At least he hoped that's what he said. Hopefully, he didn't say "To the bathroom."

The guards looked at each other, and then looked back at Freddy. A guard drew his sword, slowly. Freddy's heart sunk, as he looked around for an escape. He took a step back, as the sword slowly came his way. In the brief few seconds, he wondered if the sword was moving faster than he saw it, like when people are in car accidents, and they see the whole thing moving slower than it really is.

Freddy braced for what he thought was going to be a blow with a very heavy looking sword, when the guard spoke.

"Take this with you, in case they become unruly." The guard smiled.

Freddy tried to not look surprised and said thank you—he almost mistakenly said it in English, because the situation had scared him so. He took the sword, and quickly headed up the road to the school.

The entrance was open, and Freddy began his scouting mission. All the classroom doors were closed, and Freddy couldn't hear any talking. He zigzagged through each hall, quickly running to each classroom door, and looking in to see if there was anyone in the room. He started at the third floor, the top floor, and worked his way down, until he finally reached the ground floor, where the gym and cafeteria were located. He could hear a low murmuring and figured the hostages were being held there. Carrying a sword, a Mongol sword, no less, only gave credibility to his appearance, so he really wasn't worried about being spotted by Mongol guards.

Freddy peeked in the gym, and saw that it was full of people. They were crowded on the bleachers and the floor, or trying to sleep in the corners of the gym. Freddy walked through the gym, and everyone in the gym fell silent. He could feel the eyes of every person in the gym staring at him. He looked around and didn't see any Mongol guards. The crowd parted wherever he walked, and he headed for the back door of the gym.

Opening the door, he saw several teams of guards posted throughout the parking lot. They were well armed.

The guards were outside of the buildings, but not the inside, Freddy realized. After confirming, again, that there were no Mongols in the gym, Freddy removed his hood and spoke firmly and quietly, yet loud enough that the group could hear him.

"My name is Freddy, and I am not one of them. I am of Mongol descent, but was born and raised right here in Verona. I graduated from this school, and I still live here. Some of you may know my dad; he tends bar at the Rivertowne." Freddy paused and waited for a reaction.

Finally, an elderly man said, "Oh yeah, I know Fred from the Rivertowne. Good guy."

Once Freddy's Verona authenticity was confirmed, the group formed a circle around him.

"I have to be brief, here, but I need all of you to stay strong and be ready. An army is waiting to invade Verona and retake it—"

"What army? The US Army?" a woman asked.

"Yes, an army comprised of our US Army and Washington state citizens will be returning to the island within twenty-four hours to retake it. I need all of you to stay where you are, and do not try to escape. We need to know where everyone is when we return. We'll be back soon, I promise, and we will need your help."

Freddy looked around at the group. They looked happy about the news, but were trying to keep their happiness under wraps.

"I need you to do two things right now. One: send someone across the hall to the cafeteria and tell them what I just told you. Two: pretend this never happened. Act like you did before I got here, okay?" The group nodded in agreement, and Freddy headed out the back door.

Just as he was leaving, he turned around, and walked back toward the group. He approached the elderly man, and gave him the Mongol sword.

"Here, you take this. You'll need it soon." The man smiled and nodded.

Once outside and facing the football field, he saw scores of goats and horses grazing on the lush grass. The Mongol guards calmly watched the animals, as if they were back home, and it was just any other day.

"How arrogant", Freddy thought, "for them to think that we're going to give up so easily."

Over the next few hours, Freddy followed the same format at the Verona Bank and Riverview Park. Each time, he found the outside of each area guarded, and the inside unguarded. Each time, his fellow Veronaites were imprisoned somewhere in the building. He told all of them to stay strong and be ready to help in the retaking of Verona. The army only counted on its troops, plus the LARP army. They hadn't figured on an island full of angry Veronaites ready to fight their captors for their freedom.

The island had suffered some damage at the hand of the Mongols. As Freddy walked through the woods, he could see teams of Mongols using axes to chop down the telephone poles that lined the roads. Among the Mongol destruction teams were Veronaites who were being forced to destroy the island against their will. The pole would fall, sparks would fly, and the team would move on to the next pole. The roads were littered with them, like rotting corpses on a battlefield. Freddy passed Verona Power & Light, which supplied the island with its power. The building was a smoldering ruin.

As Dennis reported earlier, the lone cell phone tower had been downed, probably by cannon balls. Verona Water & Sewage was just a heap of brick and glass. Most houses were still standing, but, because of their conveniences, would be destroyed. Who would have ever thought that the houses in Verona, some of them a hundred years old, would be thought of as modern conveniences?

Walking past the Mongols undetected, or unbothered, was becoming a game. Freddy saw them patrolling the main roads and back streets on horseback, carrying composite bows, swords, shields, and other medieval weapons. Because of his appearance, he blended into the scenery. Freddy laughed or smiled to himself every time he passed by a Mongol guard unmolested. If they only knew what was coming.

Freddy made his way back to the other side of the island, got in his boat, and returned to the mainland. He had a lot to report to the army waiting in Uniontown. .

CHAPTER 14

Freddy arrived safely back at Uniontown (no harassment from the MP at the Hulton bridge, this time) eager to share what he saw with his fellow soldiers. When he arrived at Eiler's, he saw the LARP army going through drills using the real weapons they had acquired. They were practicing, with their military counterparts, in the fields that surrounded the hotel, and in the parking lot.

The US Army looked more professional, but the intensity of the LARP army couldn't be matched. Naturally, the LARPers were creating scenarios, rolling on the ground, battling in different positions, all the while remembering they were all on the same team. There was no longer a Verona versus Oakmont, or Penn Hills versus South Hills. There was just one army with one cause—freedom for the people of Verona.

Freddy noticed a knight in full armor off in the distance, furiously battling two other LARPers. His skill with a sword was remarkable, and he was easily handling his opponents.

Freddy walked a little closer to get a better view, and within seconds the two LARPers were on the ground, and the knight was standing victoriously over them. Freddy was surprised that they had gone down so easily. This wasn't the first time the defeated LARPers lifted a sword and shield. As the armored knight took off his helmet and helped them up, the clear features of Ed Serling were visible.

Freddy, surprised at the knight's identity, said, "Governor? Ed?"

Ed turned to face Freddy. "Freddy! Glad you made it back. Are you okay?"

Freddy, still amazed at Ed's competency with a sword, said, "Yeah, fine. Are you?"

Ed smiled broadly. "Yep, never better. Wish I could say the same for these guys!" he said, jokingly, to his opponents. Ed could see that Freddy was surprised at his skill, and added, "Yeah I had my wife overnight my armor so I'd be properly attired. And I still keep in fighting shape, you know, just in case."

"Yeah, I can tell," Freddy replied.

"Well, look, here's the plan," Ed continued "We're going to have a big dinner and go over everything for tomorrow. First, we need to debrief on everything that you saw on the island. So let's go and find Mark, Dennis, Jen, and the general.

As they walked away, Ed playfully called out to the LARPers who were waiting to spar with him, "I guess you'll have to wait to get another shot at the most powerful man in the state of Washington!"

As Freddy walked through the fields with Serling, he was amazed at how well the LARPers were handling their weapons. Real weapons were much heavier than the fiberglass-based foam ones they used in the LARP league, but it looked as if the LARPers easily adjusted to the difference. They looked prepared, and ready to prove they were capable of meeting any challenge.

Freddy was sure that there were people in the US chain of command who thought that having a group of untrained civilians take on an invading army was not only a ridiculous idea, but a dangerous one. And quite honestly, it was. But Freddy felt confident that the desire to prove themselves by taking the island back would more than make up for their military inadequacies.

He found Dennis, Mark, and Jen going over drills in a nearby part of the field. Jen saw him first, and ran over and hugged him. Dennis and Mark followed with hugs, which was unusual for both of them.

"So how's it going?" Freddy asked them.

"Pretty smooth," Dennis said, with a reassuring nod.

"Everyone has been working together all day. And, no one has used these really sharp swords to cut Mark to pieces, which is pretty amazing," Jen said with a smile. Mark rolled his eyes at her.

"Anyway," Mark said, "The weaponry is obviously much

weightier than what we're used to, and I wouldn't have used some of the wrappings on the swords had I been in charge of making the weapons, as they could easily become slippery if they get wet," he could feel the others glaring at him, and became aware of what he was doing, "But . . . we'll adapt."

Just then, the general's voice came over the hotel's outdoor PA system. "Please report to the restaurant for dinner. The food will be served in twenty minutes."

Ed turned to Freddy and said, "Let's get you in to see the general before dinner starts."

As they were walking in, Jen asked, "Hey, do you think the non-LARPers at the hotel here have any idea what we're doing? I mean, do you think they'll report it to the local news or something before we get to the island?"

"Nah," Dennis said, "we'd be out here running around in the field before a LARP battle anyway. To them, it's just us being ourselves, a bunch of weirdoes in armor chasing each other with swords for no good reason."

The group laughed at the last line, because, this time, there was a very good reason behind their actions.

The group headed into a side entrance of the hotel and met up with General Cassady in his room. Freddy told the group about everything he'd observed on the island. Cemented on the faces of his friends was a resolve to make the mission a success. The general took a few notes, and then gave out each team leader's assignments for the next day.

The restaurant's layout was changed for the occasion. There was a long table at the front of the room, with six places set, and a podium with a microphone. Two nameplates shone on the table, one for Governor Serling and one for General Cassady. As everyone headed in, the governor signaled for Mark, Freddy, Dennis, and Jen to sit at the head table with him and General Cassady.

It was a buffet-style dinner, and after everyone got their food, the general addressed the group.

"Hello, everyone. For those of you who don't know me, my name is General Cassady, and I am the ranking US military official in the state of Washington. I am stationed at nearby Fort Lewis. I became a participant in the resolution of this situation through my daughter Jen, who is a member of the Verona LARP faction. I'll be brief here, because there are other people who need to speak, but I want to say this: I have spoken to the Commander-in-Chief, and I want to assure all of you that you have the full confidence and support of the country. He wanted me to tell all of you that he is grateful for your willingness to help your fellow Americans in their time of need, and that it is Americans like you who are responsible for maintaining our freedom."

The crowd erupted in applause. The general raised his hand to quiet them down.

"Thank you, thank you . . . now, let me say this: if there is even a hint, a whiff, that this is going bad for our side, I have our troops from Fort Lewis heading toward Verona right now. If needed, they will be on the island in minutes. We will not hang you out to dry." The crowd applauded again. "Thank you. And now, a few words from Governor Ed Serling."

The governor stood up, shook hands with the general, and took the podium.

"Thank you, General, for your support. On behalf of my fellow LARPers, I appreciate it." The crowd laughed and applauded at the idea of their governor fighting alongside them as a LARPer.

"I'll be as brief as I can here, because the food is good and we all need to get to bed early tonight. Our objective for you tomorrow is this: we are not sending you to Verona to be killing machines. We want you to capture, or aid in the capture, of as many Mongols as possible. There will be two types of teams in Verona; warriors and the capture team. Each team will have a leader who will be informed of vital places on the island, and all the leaders are from Verona, which will help out when it comes to getting to the places we need to be in a timely manner. The rest of the Verona natives will be divided up into each group to provide additional help with direction.

"Each warrior leader will have a government issue two-way

radio so that they can radio the capture teams and let them know how many Mongols to expect. The warrior teams will battle the Mongols, subdue them, and then the capture teams will move in and ship the Mongols off to the cargo ships. We understand that the Mongols used boat-like carriages to transport the people of Verona to their current holding places. We are going to capture and use those same carriages to transport the Mongols to our cargo boat and off the island. Once our invasion begins, we will surround the island with US military cargo ships. So they'll already be in place, all you have to do is load 'em up. Are there any questions?"

A few seconds elapsed before a hand went up. "So are we allowed to be . . . um . . . physically aggressive toward the Mongols?"

"Yes, of course," the governor said. "We want you to protect yourself and your team. But, we don't expect you to go over there and start chopping off heads, either. Remember, follow your team leader. Round up the Mongols, get them on the carriage, and send them to the cargo ships. By the way, the team leaders are sitting here at the table with me. Mark, Dennis, and Freddy are Verona natives. The general's daughter, Jen, and myself will lead the other teams. Before I close, let me say this: as a semi-retired LARPer, I know that you are more than a bunch of weekend warriors. You are not ordinary civilians—you are a well-trained army of Americans. Freddy just got back from Verona, and he has a few things to say. Thank you."

Freddy stood up and approached the podium. Clearing his throat, he spoke, nervously, and a bit too quiet.

"I'm really not used to doing this . . . I work in an office, in a cube, so I never really have to talk to people."

The crowd chuckled.

"Like the governor . . . Ed . . . said, I am from Verona and I just got back from there. I went over to check things out so that we would have a good idea of what's over there tomorrow. My dad is over there, and he is a HAM radio operator. Last night," Freddy's voice trembled, "last night, I was lucky enough to catch him broadcasting. He somehow snuck his radio into the Kiss plant, and was able to get out a broadcast to anyone who was listening. He was able to tell everyone who was listening what it's like over there. When I was over there, I saw that everything he said was right . . . there are Mongols on the island, and most of the people of Verona are being held in the Kiss plant, the high school, the bank, and the park. I went to each place and saw them. I told all of them to be strong and to be ready. Something none of us considered is that there's an island full of people who are ready and willing to help us battle for their independence. I got to see . . . to feel . . . firsthand how ready they are.

"Since I'm of Mongolian descent, a group of them thought I was an invader, and pummeled me until they realized I was one of them. Believe me, they're ready. The island isn't in as bad a shape as I thought . . . some buildings are gone, burned to the ground, but not all of them. Buildings . . . what are buildings, anyway? It's the people who matter. And from what I saw, they're mostly okay."

Freddy's voice got stronger as he spoke. He knew he had to emphasize his next point, but he couldn't become too emotional and lose his focus.

"They're okay for now . . . but we have . . . we've got to . . . get over there tomorrow morning and free as many as possible and capture . . . or kill . . . as many invaders as we can. With every day that passes, we get closer to losing more of Verona. What is lost now can be replaced, but I don't know if we'd be able to say the same thing three days from now, or a week from now. On behalf of Verona, I want to thank all of you for your help. I know that not everyone out there is from Verona, and I know that you're really taking a chance for a bunch of people that you don't even know. But, it's something that needs to be done . . . so, thank you."

Everyone applauded, and the general took the podium one more time.

"Thank you, Governor and Freddy. Everyone, be ready, be suited up and armed, in the parking lot tomorrow at 0500. We're going to use the early hour to our advantage.

Freddy took his seat next to Dennis and began eating. The

warm, honeyed slices of ham tasted like a gourmet meal after the day that Freddy had. He eagerly dug into the meal, wanting to finish eating so that he could get to bed early.

As he was eating, Dennis asked, "So it wasn't that bad, then?"

Freddy stopped and thought for a moment, then answered as he kept cutting pieces of his ham.

"Not as bad as I thought, but enough that it hurt me to see what I saw." Freddy then paused, and looked at Dennis "I saw my dad."

"You did? Why didn't he come back with you?" Dennis asked.

"He wouldn't leave the others. I practically begged him to come back with me. It would have been easy to get him past the Mongols, since he looks like them. But he wouldn't leave. He said it was important to stay there and broadcast when he could to let us know what was happening. Which reminds me, I gotta go to my car and get my radio. I want to keep it nearby in case he's able to broadcast again."

"Did you see Brad?" Dennis asked, hesitantly.

Freddy hadn't even thought to look for Brad. Brad was such a thorn in Dennis's side most of the time that Freddy had blocked out Brad's existence.

"Um, no, I didn't. But I'm sure he's okay. I didn't see signs that anyone had been killed."

Dennis nodded in optimistic agreement.

"I tell you what, though, the first place I'm going to is the Kiss plant," said Freddy. "That's where my dad is. The general put me in charge of the team that is going to the plant. I'm going directly there, soon as my feet touch the beach on Verona. And God help anyone who gets in my way. I had to leave my dad there once. I'm not gonna do it again."

"I'm headed to the school, Jen is going to the bank, and Mark is going to the park," Dennis responded. "I wonder where Ed is going?"

"He's going to be our decoy," Mark said, overhearing the conversation. "Ed's team is going to take the Mongols on, head on, so that we can get to our destinations and free as many as we can. He's also gonna use his team to help manage the transfer of the Mongols to the cargo ships."

It was nearing the end of the dinner, and the LARPers were filing out of the restaurant to their rooms. Tomorrow, the liberation of Verona would begin. And, hopefully, it would end with the freedom of the citizens of Verona.

Freddy, Dennis, Mark, and Jen headed to their rooms and slept soundly. General Cassady and Governor Serling were up a little later than everyone else, finalizing plans. As the general said, the US Army would be waiting nearby in the event things went awry in Verona, and he had to make sure that everything was in place for tomorrow. After making a few phone calls, including a call to the president, Governor Serling spent the remainder of the evening polishing his armor and weapons, before retiring for the night.

CHAPTER 15

It was one of those mornings when you wake up feeling like you just fell into bed.

Freddy, Dennis, and Mark woke up at 4:00 a.m., but there wasn't too much talk between the lifelong friends, if for no other reason than the early hour.

Before they left the room to head to the parking lot, Mark was in a solemn mood. "Hey, guys, look . . . um . . . if things don't go well and something happens—"

Dennis put his hand on Mark's shoulder and said, confidently, "Nothing is going to happen to anyone . . . nothing. We're going to go over there, take our home back, and kick them out. Tonight, we'll be sleeping back home in Verona."

"Yeah, but—" Mark protested.

"No buts!" Freddy said. "I didn't risk my life over there yesterday for there to be any buts. You'll be just as strong, courageous and alive as the rest of. Now grab your weapons and let's go."

Mark nodded. The three friends knew how much the day meant, and how much they meant to each other. Today would be a day they would share with their children and grandchildren.

At 5:00 a.m., all the LARPers were in the parking lot in full gear ready to liberate Verona. General Cassady came out of the hotel, flanked by Jen and Governor Serling. The general climbed onto the hood of the nearest car and addressed the crowd.

"I want to thank everyone for being prompt. A sign of a good army is one that is ready to go, and you are clearly ready to go."

The crowd responded with applause and shouts of support.

The general continued, "We are on the brink of American history right now. It's been over 200 years since Americans have bonded together to fight off an enemy invader whose goal is to claim our land for themselves. And we all know what happened the last time someone tried it!" The crowd roared its approval.

"And I think we all know what's going to happen this time, too."

The LARPers were so loud in their enthusiasm that the general had to ask them to quiet down. "Please, please, just give me another minute. I'm just as excited as you are. We will be parking near the entrance of the Hulton Bridge. Once there, you will be given a number, one through five. Please board the cargo ship with the corresponding number. Your number is your team. Stick with your team and follow your team leader. By our count, there are thirty people among us who are from Verona. If you are one of these people, you do not need a number. Divide yourselves up in groups of six, and board a cargo boat. We want to keep the Verona natives evenly separated so that they can help direct the rest of the team once we get to the island. Thank you, Americans, and we'll see you at the bridge."

Everyone headed to their cars with a strong spirit and confident will. The irony wasn't lost on any of them that they had gone through their lives being mocked by society for their love of LARP, and now, they were going to save that very same society.

The army traveled in a caravan, with the military vehicles at the front and rear. General Cassady called ahead to alert all necessary police personnel of their arrival. The roads were cleared, streets blocked, and detours established, so the army could get to Verona quickly, without having to stop anywhere.

They were one caravan, one army, one force, heading to one destination, to accomplish one goal.

In many ways, this was fantasy fulfillment for all of them; saviors coming in the dawn of the day, in a big rumbling caravan, to rescue society. It's what they had read about in books for decades, and a scenario they had played out in their minds, endlessly, their entire lives.

"Who says LARP isn't reality?" Mark asked Dennis, rhetorically.

As they traveled the final mile down the long hill that is Hulton Road, to Hulton Bridge, the area looked abandoned, almost like a ghost town. Familiar sights had vanished. For the first time in their lives, Hulton Road, one of the centers of

[139]

business for the area, was empty. None of the businesses were open, and the traffic lights flashed hauntingly between red, yellow, and green, along the deserted streets. The houses were dark, and an eerie silence strangled the entire area. It was more than empty. It was dead.

The members of the caravan felt a creepy, apocalyptical chill to their core as they stepped out of their vehicles, and looked around.

General Cassady was greeted with a very respectful salute from the local army company protecting the bridge. The general saluted back and said, "Good job," to the officer.

"We evacuated everyone and everything within a five mile radius. There's absolutely nothing for a long way. If things get ugly, it gives us some room to play with," said the officer.

"Well done," the general responded, as the officer tried to hide his pleasure at the compliment. "Are the boats ready?"

"Yes, sir, they are ready to go."

"How about the backup teams?"

"They are in place, sir, awaiting your word, if necessary."

"Good. Good."

"Is there anything else, sir?" the officer asked.

"Yes, have your team help ours safely board the ships."

"Yes, sir," the officer said, saluting and turning away.

Designated officials handed out numbers one through five, and the unit at the bridge was assisting everyone with getting onto the right boat. Surprisingly, or maybe not so surprisingly, the LARPers eagerly headed for the boats. Everyone stood in line with their tickets, waiting to go on a boat ride. It looked like an amusement park.

The reality of the situation became clearer, as everyone made their way to the boats. They could smell the smoke from the fires and a gray cloud hovered over the island. The stench of Verona's struggle for life was hard to endure, mentally and physically.

Dennis and Freddy walked together to their boats.

"Guess this is it, huh?" Dennis said.

"Damn right it is," Freddy said, determination in his voice.

As they waited in line to board their boat, they saw Mark coming down the path. He was holding his cell phone to his face.

"It's dawn and we're about to commence operations," he said, focused and serious. "The historic event is about to occur. Operation LARP is in full force. I'll check back with all of you once it's over. And don't forget to check my business site. All Mongolian Death Worm battle toys are half off, now through the end of the week. Vollrath, out."

Dennis and Freddy looked at each other in disbelief.

"What are you doing?" Freddy asked, accusingly.

"Nothing . . . just . . . um . . . updating my video blog on Youface, that's all."

Dennis turned his head, shaking it in disgust.

Freddy spoke for both of them. "Are you nuts? We have a major military operation about to go down, and you're telling the world???"

"I can't even believe this," Dennis said.

"No, wait, it's not like that," Mark sputtered, trying to recover. "I didn't give any specifics, but it will serve as an important historical document, and will probably help to land me a major book deal once this is all over."

Freddy looked at Dennis, and, as if Freddy said something subliminally, Dennis replied, "It is what it is."

Trying to lighten the mood, Dennis said to Mark, "Just don't try any of that Vollrath crap over there. It ain't gonna work."

Mark looked over at Freddy and Dennis. "Yeah, I know. Besides, I have something better planned."

"Aw, c'mon, don't even go there. We can't . . ." Dennis said, suddenly stopping. They were on the shore now, and about to board their boats when the three of them saw Verona for the first time, together. Flames burned. The familiar scenery and skyline was erased. The struggling vision of Verona filled their senses.

"Wow," Mark said, quietly. Dennis exhaled heavily, and Freddy said nothing. After looking for a moment, Freddy turned his head away, clenched his fists, and boarded his boat.

The army was going to use the same tactic they used when

Freddy went on his reconnaissance mission. They would send a few decoys to the front of the island to draw the attention of the Mongols, while the rest of the boats would head around to the back of the island, charge the shore, and head to their destinations led by their Veronaite leaders.

The river water looked black in the dawn, as the decoys went out first to the left, while the troops headed right, to the back of the island. Almost immediately, the Mongols began firing cannonballs at the decoys. The decoys fired back, not really trying to hit the Mongols, but close enough to cause the Mongols to retaliate. A few times, the Mongol shots came very close to hitting the decoys, missing the ships by mere feet. When it appeared that the Mongols were focused on the decoys, the troops headed to the island.

In less than an hour, the sun would rise. The army had to make it to the island to begin their mission, before the sun came up. Surprise was a key element here, and would hopefully make up for the lack of battle experience on the part of the LARP army.

As everyone headed over to Verona, the leaders of each group on all the boats spread the same message—stay alert, stay together, and follow your leaders.

There was silence from the LARP army as the boats quickly headed over to Verona. The farther they got from shore, the stronger the reality became that they were headed into a real battle with a real enemy who would try to kill them, for real. Teachers, garbage men, bank tellers, retail workers and managers, and I.T. people were on a US Army cargo ship heading off to war. Just last weekend they were running through their respective battlefields, shouting spells at one another, and getting hit with fiberglass swords.

The boats landed without incident, and the LARP army stormed the beach as quietly as possible.

Each area was chosen based on the likelihood that it held Veronaite hostages. The armies dispersed as planned, and everyone headed to their designated areas. .

CHAPTER 16

Freddy aggressively took his faction to the Kiss plant, where he had seen his father just twelve hours before. He was moving through the woods of Verona so quickly that some of his team had trouble keeping up with him, but Freddy felt strong enough, and angry enough, to take on whoever was waiting for him.

Freddy waited for his team to catch up as he approached the back end of the Kiss plant. When everyone arrived, he looked them over, trying to tune out the huffing and puffing. His eyes focused on the group, and he spoke with authority.

"Here's what's happening. I was just here a few hours ago, and there are people being held in the storage areas of the plant. Those of you who live here know the plant like the back of your hand. Divide yourselves up into small groups, and each group head for a storage area. Free the people in the area, and have them help you in subduing the Mongols inside, if there are any. I'm gonna climb up the back here, go through the window, and let you in the back door. As soon as you see me enter in the window, quietly head down this hill to the back door. Questions?"

Freddy's intensity almost prohibited questions. His team knew that they had to be as intense as he was, otherwise they'd possibly face the same fate as the Mongols they were about to meet.

Freddy headed down the hill to the plant, taking huge frog leaps. He made it down the hill in less than ten leaps, and hit the ground running. In seconds, he was scaling the wall, and climbing through the window. Before he landed on the inside floor of the plant, he looked around to see if the situation had changed. It hadn't. There still weren't any Mongol guards near the storage areas, and he assumed that they were stationed outside the front gate, as they were at his last visit. Freddy landed on the floor quietly, and ran to open the back door.

Which set off the alarm.

For some reason, the Mongols hadn't cut the electricity that powered the alarm. Or maybe it was the battery back-up that powered the warning sign. Either way, the Mongols would be in the area within seconds.

Freddy quickly opened the door and saw a look of fear on the faces of his team, who were right outside the door, waiting to come in. They expected to come in, free the hostages, and slip out unnoticed. Instead, they could hear warlike yelling coming at them, and the stomping of boots, from the front of the building.

Freddy took charge.

"Half of you, come and fight with me. The other half, work on freeing the hostages. Once they're free, they'll be more than ready to join the fight."

Freddy drew his weapons, a Morningstar and a sword, and ran toward the violent noise that was only getting louder. Half of the team drew their weapons and followed him, the other half headed for the storage areas.

About thirty Mongols ran toward Freddy and his troop. The Mongols seemed a bit confused at first, because they were fighting an army that looked like them. The LARP army had no such confusion, because they knew the enemy, at least in an abstract sense. Freddy thought of his beloved dad with every swing of his weapon. He thought of his dad, holed up in a stinking storage locker for the last few days, wondering if, or how, he'd ever get out. Freddy tried to drive the sparkling, studded ball through the enemy with every swing. For every other day of his adult life, Freddy was small, American born, and spent most of his day sitting behind a desk. But today he was a Mongol, a true Mongol, not a terrorist.

As he fought, he looked around to check on his team. He smiled as he saw Lenny, the local mailman, wailing away with a club, on a Mongol.

Better for Lenny to go postal here than at work, he thought.

Within minutes, Freddy heard more people coming. He turned to the door, ready to battle more Mongols, when he saw something else.

He saw his dad, running out of the storage area, followed by a gang of angry Veronaites.

They had wrenches, glass bottles, hammers, things found lying around in a plant. When the Mongols still standing saw who, and what, was coming at them, a blanket of fear covered them. Freddy ran for his dad, who embraced him.

"Now, son, now, we will fight!" his dad exclaimed. Both men turned together, and ran to the nearest group of Mongols.

The whole confrontation lasted less than ten minutes. All of the Mongols were beaten so badly, that they were either unconscious, or too battered to move. The LARP army exchanged high-fives and hugs all around. Freddy, his arm around his dad, picked up his two-way radio and said, "This is team leader Freddy. I'm at the Kiss plant and need a pickup. Got about thirty semi-conscious Mongols here."

A static voice replied, "Will they offer resistance when picked up?"

Freddy laughed. "No, I'm sure they'll be thrilled to get out of here."

"We'll be there in ten minutes," the voice answered.

Freddy hugged his dad again, and said, "I was so worried about you. If something had happened to you—"

"Well, it didn't, so don't even think that way. I'm a little hungry, and a little tired, but doing okay." Fred Sr. was quiet for a moment, as he studied his son's face. "Son, I'm so proud of you. I can never repay you for what you did today."

"Dad, of course I would—"

"No," Freddy Sr. said, softly, but emphatically. "You are a hero today. Today you helped to save Verona, and help to clear the name of our people. I know your grandparents would be so proud of you right now."

Freddy looked away, trying to conceal his tears, and nodded.

The capture team showed up, and began handcuffing, and dragging, the defeated Mongols out of the plant.

"Why don't you head back with them, Dad?" Freddy asked.

"Well, what are you going to do?" his father responded.

"I'm gonna join up with another team. There's more work to

be done."

"You're not going without me. This is my home too, you know."

Freddy could tell that trying to convince his dad to head back to safety with the capture team would be a waste of time, so he just smiled and handed his dad his Morningstar. "Know how to use it?" Freddy asked with a smile.

"I think I can figure it out," his dad said.

Freddy looked out at the LARP army, and the newly freed Veronaites. Eyes were bruised, as were jaws, and limbs. Scratches, cuts, and torn clothes were scattered among the LARP warriors.

"Is everyone all right? Any major injuries?"

"Yeah, I got a problem," a voice came from the back. It was Mookie, the local Verona tattoo artist. His bulging biceps were covered in tattoos, and his beard covered his chest. No one knew his real name. He was just Mookie.

"What's wrong, Mook?" Freddy asked, concerned.

"I ain't kicked enough Mongol butt today!" Mookie said, full of adrenaline.

"Mookie . . . Mookie . . . Mookie," the army chanted.

Freddy grinned. "Well, let's see what we can do about that! Okay, those of you who would like to go back with the capture team, feel free to do so. I appreciate your support. Those of you who want to stay, I am going to the bank now to help Jen's team."

The senior citizens, and the children, and mothers, went with the capture team.

"Those of you who have more than one weapon, please share with those around you. Also, feel free to grab anything that you feel you can use on your way out."

Freddy's team swelled from around twenty to about fifty. After re-arming themselves and grabbing some delicious Kiss beverages, they headed to the bank to help Jen. .

CHAPTER 17

The huge Roman-style pillars, that guarded the entrance of the Verona Bank, were a dirty gray color, covered in a century's worth of grime. The lobby was lined with yellowed, twenty-five-cent bubblegum machines, which emanated a fruity bubblegum smell.

From the entrance to the lobby, there was a huge vault at the far end of the bank, parallel to the front door. The right side was lined with teller windows, where generations of Veronaites had done their banking, and the left side was lined with small cubicles, where the same people had taken out mortgages.

The tiled floors had an aged tint from years of bright summer sunlight shining through the windows, and the air of the bank smelled musty, like a combination of the fruity gum, and the history of the building itself.

The bank was located in the "business district" of Verona, which stretched roughly five blocks. There were businesses here and there on side streets, but the majority of Verona commerce happened in this area. The commerce district was just a long, straight road—Verona road—with businesses on either side of the street, and two stop lights to regulate traffic. A huge billboard with a full-color painting of an old-fashioned paddlewheel boat sat at the corner of First Street and Verona Road.

The billboard proudly boasted—*Verona: The Spot That's More Than A Dot. Established 1871.*

As was the case with most of Verona, whatever plot of land wasn't occupied by a building was occupied by woods. Jen's team crept down the hill of First Street, which ran parallel to Verona road. Their target was the roof of Della Salla's Pizza, which was across the street from the bank. They would get to the roof, and, using binoculars, scout the area surrounding the bank, so that they could enter safely, and free the hostages in the bank cellar.

As the team made it to the roof, the famous Della Salla's Pizza aroma enveloped them. Della Salla's pizza was a tradition that Veronaites had ingested for more than sixty years.

Jen crouched down, behind the trademark Della Salla's sign—the Italian boot covered in cheese, with pepperoni marking important Italian cities—and focused her binoculars.

"Looks like around forty or fifty of them within the few blocks of here" she reported.

"We've got twenty with us," came the whispered reply from a team member.

"Yeah," Jen responded, acknowledging the mathematical issue.

Lieutenant Nick Landolina, specially assigned to Jen by General Cassady, called the unit into a circle and spoke to them, quietly. "We're outnumbered here by about two-to-one, at least. We've got two choices: call for backup, or try to get in, and get out, without getting noticed. Ms. Cassady, I have to say that your father would probably want us to call for backup."

"What if the backup gets caught, or draws attention to our position?" asked Mitch, a retired mechanic. His broad shoulders suggested he could handle a problem, if it came up. But not everyone had that advantage.

Lt. Landolina nodded. "It's possible."

"I say we just go in," Matt said. "If we hold off any longer, the Mongols might hurt the hostages."

Jen took a moment to evaluate the situation, and everyone's position. "I respect your position, Lieutenant," Jen said, diplomatically, "but we can't call for backup. I agree with Mitch, it's too risky. There are people in that bank waiting for us, and we're here."

Landolina reluctantly nodded.

Jen continued, "What we need to do, then, is have a small team, around five, go into the bank and free the people inside. The rest of us will stand guard outside. Those of you standing guard have to stay hidden, though. Only come out if the Mongols approach the bank. Does anyone see any problems?"

"Well, man, the problem is—" began Jeff, the manager of

the Verona bowling alley, who stopped in mid-sentence, when he heard the rustling in the woods behind him.

Jen drew her long dagger, Mitch stood up, pulling a long, heavy wrench out of his back pocket. Some of the other team members drew their weapons, while others were frozen in fear.

A small, hooded figure landed on the roof of Della Salla's and looked around. Jen stood up, prepared for battle.

The hooded figure put his finger to his lips, slowly removing his hood. It was Freddy. He signaled for his team to quietly descend to the roof. They slowly made their way down, crouching as they landed. Everyone stayed low to avoid being seen by the Mongols on the street below.

"Thought you could use some company," Freddy said to Jen.

"Thank God. We were just about to go in, but we're outnumbered," Jen replied, relieved.

"Now they're outnumbered," Freddy said triumphantly, as his team continued to descend to the roof.

Jen looked over the team, which now stood at around seventy. "New plan," she announced. "I'll take ten into the bank with me. The rest of you, go kick some invader butt!"

Freddy smiled and nodded. He turned to his team, and said quietly, "Instead of running at them like a bunch of amateurs, we'll divide up, and come down from the streets that intersect Verona Road. That way, we'll surround 'em, and hit them from all sides. They won't be able to escape. Anyone object?"

Everyone nodded in agreement.

"Good," Freddy said. "Split yourselves up in groups of ten, and start heading for the intersecting streets. We'll all begin coming down to Verona Road in ten minutes." Freddy grabbed his two-way radio to contact the capture team. "Team leader Freddy here. We'll need a pickup of about fifty near Della Salla's in about thirty minutes . . . or less," Freddy said, making a joking reference to the pizza place's slogan.

"Got it," a voice answered. "We'll be there."

"Don't head to the bank until you see us come down, all right?" Freddy said to Jen.

"Right, got it," Jen replied.

[149]

Freddy smiled and ran up the hill with his team, energized by their first victory at the Kiss plant. It was kind of like boxing—you're scared of getting hit until you take your first punch. After that, your fear is conquered, and you're ready to fight. With the invasion of the Kiss plant, the LARP army had taken their first punch. Now they knew what a real battle was, what would happen, and what it took to win. The fear was gone, and they could taste freedom, and victory, as if it were a garlicky slice of Della Salla's pizza.

Jen and her team waited until they saw and heard Freddy's team attacking the Mongols. The Mongols were totally caught off-guard. They were just milling around in the intersection near the bank. They were armed, but unsuspecting. Once Jen saw that the Mongols were occupied, she and her team headed into the bank. As at the Kiss plant, the guards were outside of the hostage areas, not inside. Jen headed for the bank vault, figuring that the hostages were in there. The vault was locked, and she obviously didn't know the combination.

"I know there are people here, so where are they?" she asked her team. "We better sweep the bank. Someone look for the door to the attic. I'll find the basement."

She took a few team members to the back of the bank, while the other team members began looking for the attic door. After a few minutes of kicking down the office doors of the bank president and vice president, she found the door to the basement. There was a faint, unidentifiable sound coming from somewhere. For all she knew, it could have been Mongols waiting to ambush anyone who went down there. She flipped the light switch, forgetting that all the power on the island had been cut, and then hollered down into the blackness of the basement.

"Anybody down there?"

There was silence, as if her call had difficulty penetrating the darkness, then a reply.

"Here, we're down here!"

"Okay, we're coming!" she yelled down. Turing to Walt, a team member, she commanded, "Go get the others. Tell them we found everyone, and need them here."

[150]

Jen, and the rest of her team, slowly descended the creaky steps to the basement. The basement was musty, and smelled like old money, and mildew. There were a few small windows in the basement, which provided fleeting rays of light, enough to see that the hostages were in jail-like cells. The bank was built around 1920, and the cells were probably used to store and protect important documents and paperwork, before the advent of electronic records.

The hostages were held in the cells, which were beyond overcrowded. There was a row of cells on either side of the basement. Jen stood in the middle of the hall, just looking at the people, people she usually saw walking the streets of Verona, when she visited Freddy, Dennis, and Mark.

The pungent odor of people trapped in cages for several days overtook Jen, and she covered her nose with her shirt. As she looked around for a way to open the cages, she saw sick, hungry people, desperate to get out.

It was shock, more than anything else, to see men, women, and children in cages. Realizing she was gawking, Jen quickly snapped out of it, and shouted, "Does anyone know where the keys are?"

"No," a voice from one of the cells said. "They take the keys every time they come to feed us."

Jen turned to Walt, who was an engineer. "So how are we gonna break these locks?"

Walt took a look at the lock on the nearest cell. "Well, they're pretty old, probably the original locks from when these cells were built. From what I can see, they look rusty. Bet we can just pound 'em 'til they break."

Realizing that the options were few, and that they needed to get out of the bank if Freddy was losing, Jen said, "Everyone divide up and start pounding away at the locks. Use whatever you have to try and break them."

Within seconds, the "*clank*" of metal on metal echoed throughout the dingy basement. Sparks flew, and in a few minutes, the beautiful symphony of decrepit locks crashing to the floor reverberated around the cement basement.

[151]

Once the team members began opening cell doors, the people were anxious to get out.

"Please go up the stairs quietly, and do not exit the bank. Please wait in the lobby until we all get up there safely," Jen reminded them.

As the people began heading up the steps to the lobby, an older woman approached Jen.

"Um . . . excuse me . . . I think there's something you need to know."

"Yes?" Jen replied, worried about whatever the woman was about to share.

"The Mongols aren't what you think they are," the woman said.

"What do you mean?" Jen asked, incredulously.

"They're not cruel invaders. They really don't know what they're doing," the woman said.

Jen tried to control her emotions when she answered, but knew she was coming off as hostile. "How could they not be what I think they are? They came here, took your island, put you in a cage in the basement of this bank, and now you're telling me that they're an okay group of people? Do you have Stockholm Syndrome or something?"

"My name is Inga, and I love Verona as much as anyone. I emigrated here from Germany forty years ago, and Verona has been my land of opportunity. Verona is my home. I wasn't happy about sitting in this rotten basement for the last few days, but I talked to the Mongols when they came to feed us, and they're not what you think they are."

Jen looked at Inga, dumbfounded. Trying to be diplomatic, she said, "Okay, fine. Please go upstairs so that we can get out of here."

Jen grabbed Inga's arm and began to lead her up to the lobby, when Inga indignantly broke her arm free of Jen's grasp, and became more forceful in her tone.

"I'm not going anywhere until you listen."

Inga made it clear by her body language that she meant what she said. Jen had no choice but to remain attentive.

[152]

"The Mongols are being brainwashed by a man they call The King. I don't know his real name, but that's what they call him. They're just normal people like you and me who wanted a better opportunity in life, so they came here. I can relate to that, can't you?"

Jen was silent, and continued listening to Inga.

"Why do you think it was so easy for you to get in here? Why do you think there wasn't anyone guarding us? It's because these Mongols aren't an army. They had no idea what they were getting into when they got on the boat to get here. That King maniac conned these simple people into helping him take over the island. They were able to do it because they caught us off guard. They looked scary and acted tough. Nobody in Verona ever expected to get invaded, so we had no defense, and no choice, but to get herded off into these storage areas. Had we known about it, it would have been a different story."

Jen tried to take in everything Inga had just said, but it still seemed so absurd.

"So how do you know that the Mongols aren't just conning you? Maybe they just told you that so you wouldn't fight back?"

"Because," Inga said, "I could see it in their eyes. After they captured us, they weren't aggressive toward us. Not at all. Not even a little bit. Plus, they're so unorganized. Why would a real army take an island and not protect it? They don't know how to be a conquering army, because they aren't one. The King just promised these people a better life and they were simple enough and desperate enough to believe him. They really don't know what they're doing. If they did, you wouldn't be here."

Jen could feel herself softening to Inga's words.

"Thanks for the info," she said. "I'll be sure to pass it along."

Inga slowly headed up to the lobby, holding on to the rails as she walked. Her words were still with Jen. As the last person headed up the steps, Jen followed, and closed the basement door.

The lobby was filled with people, and the LARP army took a head count. Freddy appeared in the lobby, and Jen was surprised to see him.

"What are you doing here?" she asked him, surprised.

"Just thought I'd help you out," Freddy said, puzzled at Jen's question.

"Shouldn't you be off kicking butt?" Jen asked.

"The butt has been kicked." Freddy smiled as he spoke. "We had to break a few heads, but after that, they were totally compliant. They pretty much laid down for us. The capture team is there now, loading them up. It's almost like the Mongols were happy to see us."

Jen looked over at Inga, as Freddy finished his sentence. Inga looked at her, with an "I told you so" look.

Jen related to Freddy what Inga told her, and Freddy couldn't believe it. He really didn't want to accept it, after the strong feelings he had in seeing his dad locked up at the Kiss plant. But then, it all made sense to him. The easy time he had getting into the Kiss plant, and conquering it. The effortless battle outside. He also thought of his grandparents, who were immigrants, and how they came to America, to Verona, for a better life.

"Maybe you oughta pass this info on to your dad?" Freddy said to Jen.

"Yeah, I will. When the time comes."

Just then, as the Mongols were rounded up, the surprising form of General Cassady surveyed the situation. When Lt. Landolina saw the general, he quickly approached him and saluted.

"General Cassady, we didn't expect you to be here, sir," Lt. Landolina said.

"Where's my daughter?" the general asked.

"She's in the bank, sir, with the rest of her team. Ms. Cassady expertly handled the situation, and did not sustain any injuries. With all due respect, sir, she is very much her father's daughter."

General Cassady let his guard down, and smiled. "Thank you, Nick."

"My pleasure, sir."

Since they had spent a few days in the basement of the bank, most of the hostages chose to go back to the mainland with the capture team. Freddy and Jen's teams moved on to Riverview Park to meet Mark, who always seemed to need help. .

CHAPTER 18

Riverview Park sat peacefully, beautifully, overlooking the Strait of Juan de Fuca. Most of the people who grew up in Verona spent their summers at the park, as it was the only park on the island. The lower level of the park held the playground, basketball courts, tennis courts, pavilions, and picnic grounds, with grills. There was also a track, lined with oak trees, for running, or walking. A Veronaite could spend their childhood playing at the playground, their adult years playing tennis, and their retirement walking the track.

The upper part of the park had a football field, which was converted to a baseball field in the summer. Wooden bleachers, where generations of kids carved their names, sat quietly on the sidelines. It was sort of a Verona tradition to find your parents', or grandparents', names on the bleachers, and carve your name near theirs.

Army intelligence revealed that the Mongols were centralized at Riverview Park. It made sense, really, because the park was near the water, had pavilions, and provided tree coverage, and grass, for their animals.

Mark and his unit were assigned the park as their territory, and he knew every blade of grass. He hadn't played sports there, but spent lots of time sitting in a far off corner of the park, reading books about medieval mythology.

Mark led the LARP army into the park, and hid beneath the bleachers. They wanted to get a feel of what was going on at the park, and how many Mongols were there. As Mark looked through his telescope, his unit discussed battle strategies. Once he got an idea of how many Mongols they'd be up against, and their location within the park, he turned to his unit.

"Okay, we're not gonna go in there with our swords swingin'. I've got a better idea." Mark removed a huge backpack from his shoulders as he spoke. "Everyone, please start unpacking the backpacks I gave you before we left."

The rest of the unit did what they were told, as Mark unpacked his own.

Each member of the team pulled out a funnel-like piece of material. The material was red, and easily folded, or expanded, because of the collapsible metal rings that lined each piece. The bottom of each piece had a section cut out for walking. The idea was to get into the section, standing up, and attach to another section thereby forming . . . something.

"Why am I doing this?" a team member asked, indignantly.

"Because you're going to be part of a very large Mongolian death worm," Mark said, without looking up, as he continued unpacking his bag.

"What?" said another team member, as she examined her materials.

"A Mongolian death worm," Mark said again, as if the team hadn't heard him the first time.

"What . . . what's a death snail?" someone asked.

"Worm. Mongolian death worm," Mark responded, briefly stopping his unpacking. He looked up and saw his team looking at him, bewildered.

"You're not gonna need your weapons here. The Mongolians have a legendary fear of the Mongolian death worm. It's a big red worm, a supernatural creature, sort of like their version of Bigfoot. Or I guess it would be a Yeti to the Mongols. Bigfoot is more of an American phenomenon, specifically in the Pacific Northwest. Anyway, everyone here has a six-foot piece of worm that connects to another piece of worm. We're all gonna get in our worm pieces, connect, and slither our way to the lower end of the park, which is where they're all located. Once they see us, they'll surrender."

"That is the absolute dumbest thing I've ever heard," protested a military team member. "It's not going to work. We'll all get killed in this stupid snake. I'm going to radio General Cassady, and tell him to abort your mission."

Mark was stunned. "What's so dumb about it? If you saw a Bigfoot coming at you, telling you to surrender or else, wouldn't you crap your drawers and give up?"

"No, I would either run away, or run at it, and cut it up into little pieces. And what if the Mongols decide to charge this snake, then what? We'll be defenseless in there."

Although Mark was trying to control the very thing that caused a rift between him and Dennis a few days before, namely anger and condescension, he couldn't hold it in any longer.

"It's a Mongolian death worm, you idiot, not a snake, not a snail, not a slug, but a worm. The Mongolian death worm is a feared creature in Mongolian lore, and it was believed to spit sulfuric acid, which, in case you didn't make it through eighth grade science, will kill someone. Also, since you've demonstrated no knowledge whatsoever of Mongolian mythology, the horrible Mongolian death worm is also more than capable of killing, at great distances, using a frightening electrical discharge."

"So how are you going to shoot acid at them without burning yourself?" demanded another military team member.

Mark continued, his tone unchanged. "Providing you with information is preventing me from rigging my section of the Mongolian death worm, which will contain a pressurized excretion system that shoots a harmless, yet scary, mixture of chemicals that will imitate the properties of sulfuric acid, with none of the unpleasant consequences. In addition to the scary mixture of chemicals, I have rigged a PA system to my section of the Mongolian death worm, so that I can command them to surrender. While I am moving and shooting the scary mixture of chemicals, I will launch fireworks out of the mouth of the Mongolian death worm to simulate the aforementioned deadly electrical discharge. Is there any other part of this complicated strategy that you fail to grasp?"

The team looked at Mark in stunned, confused silence.

"Good. Each of you has a number sewn into your section of the Mongolian death worm. Find the team member who is in front of you, and prepare to attach to that member. You have five minutes to find your partner, and to prepare for invasion."

As the team members milled around and matched up the

numbers, they saw their names, their parents' names, and, in some cases, their grandparents' names, carved into the bleachers.

Mark configured the various components of his section of the worm, and called out to the team.

"Everyone ready? Everyone found their partners?" The team lined up according to their assigned section number, and began assembling the worm.

On the inside, it looked like a long, red tunnel. There were no eyes, and no discernible mouth, just a black, disgusting looking exit hole. It sort of looked as if a black mop were attached in a circle around the exit hole. Everyone inside the worm was facing forward, which was a good thing, and they were trying to find their footing. Once inside, and situated, Mark turned to look at his team behind him.

"Okay, everyone, start walking forward. Small steps, right foot first."

The worm was moving. Slowly, each team member took a step, which gave the appearance of a slither. As Mark looked back, he saw determination, unity, and smiling. Even the military team members looked like they were having fun.

As the death worm slithered across the baseball field, Mark began to spray the mysterious chemical mixture from the hose that ran out of the worm's mouth. When it hit the ground, it caused the ground to smoke, giving the impression it was acid. Mark, looking through the mouth opening, saw the first group of Mongols.

They immediately began screaming, "*Allghoi!!! Allghoi!!!*" the Mongolian word for worm.

Mark turned on the PA system he had hooked up in his section of the worm. "Bow before me, infidels! Your hour has come!" He was speaking Mongolian! "On your knees, you wretched people! On your knees, surrender to me!"

The worm continued its menacing slither toward the Mongols. They were on their knees, faces to the dirt. Mark lit a few firecrackers, and threw them out of the mouth of the worm. They exploded, shooting sparks.

When the rest of the Mongol group heard the commotion,

they ran toward the noise, swords drawn. But, when they saw that it was the mythical *Allghoi*, they dropped their weapons, and screamed in fear.

Mark shot out more acid just to reinforce his power.

"Surrender or die!!!" he shouted in a deep, menacing voice. The Mongols dropped to their knees in complete surrender. He turned to his group, tossing his two-way radio to the person behind him.

"Here, call the transport team. Tell them to get here ASAP!"

"Where is your king?" Mark sternly asked, in Mongolian. When the prostrated Mongolians did not answer, he added a voice effect to his PA system, which made his voice sound deeper, and more evil. "WHERE IS YOUR KING?" "Acid" and firecrackers exploded out of the worm's mouth.

The Mongolians shrieked in terror.

Finally, a few of them shouted, "Please do not harm us, oh great *Allghoi*. Our king is on top of the hill, in the temple with the cross. Mercy, great *Allghoi*, mercy!"

Just then, the transport team arrived, and when they saw the worm, they drew their weapons. Mark kept his plan a secret, and the transport team didn't know what to make of it. He could see what was about to happen, namely, that the transport team was about to chop the worm into tiny pieces.

"Wait, wait, it's us. It's Mark and my team. Wait, we're in here!" he shouted through his PA, forgetting to turn off the evil voice effect. Realizing what he did, he said it again, this time in his normal voice.

The capture team saw the Mongols, on their knees, still face down in the dirt, and began rounding them up. Mark, turning to the team inside the worm, congratulated them on the victory, and the worm began to disassemble itself.

"That's a heckuva snake you got there," a member of the capture team said to Mark.

"It's a—never mind. Can I have your two-way please? I need to tell Ed something," Mark responded. "Ed? This is Mark. . . I found out where their king is hiding out."

"Great job," came the response. "Where is he?"

[160]

"He's at St. Joe's church, which is located at the hilltop of Verona. You can't miss it. It sits on the corner of Main Street, and it's the only church on the hilltop."

"Got it," Ed replied. "We'll send a team up there now. Thanks."

"No problem."

Mark smiled ear to ear in satisfaction as the Mongols were being rounded up and carted off the island. So far, his effort had yielded the greatest results. It looked as though there were at least seventy-five Mongols in the park who were now leaving the island, thanks to the feared Mongolian death worm. Mark had come at his mission from a different angle. Instead of using force, he used his brains.

He knew what Freddy, Dennis, and Jen had thought; he would somehow go overboard, and possibly put the whole mission in jeopardy. He was "that" guy who went over the top, not out of ego or need, but out of wanting to do things the right way. His way.

"Hey, Mark," a member of his team asked. "Where'd you learn to speak Mongolian?"

Mark felt like a celebrity, or at least a local hero, being interviewed on the news.

"Well, while we were traveling from Uniontown to here, I took an online course on my cell phone. I didn't get to finish the whole course, but I got enough of it that I could say what needed to be said. Oh, and just for the record, I was speaking the historically-correct dialect and variation applicable to the specific type of Mongols we are dealing with."

"What is that? A huge red slug?" a voice from behind asked.

Mark took a deep breath, trying to contain his frustration. "It's not a slug. It's a Mongolian death worm. I've already said that, and laid out the entire history of this fearsome beast. If you had paid attention . . ." As Mark turned, he saw the expressionless face of General Cassady.

"Oh."

"Was this your idea?" the general asked, as beads of sweat began to stream down Mark's face.

"Well, yes . . . in a way . . . mostly . . . I mean, it really isn't .
. ."

"Did you use this 'worm' to get the Mongols to surrender, without anyone getting hurt?"

Mark nervously nodded.

The general looked around at the Mongolians being rounded up. "Good job," he said, patting Mark on the shoulder. Mark jerked forward, and spit out a quick, "Thank you, sir."

"This is going better than I thought," the general said.

"Yes, sir," Mark replied. Given the chance, he would have gladly crawled back into the worm before he said something stupid.

"But you still have to stay away from my daughter."

"Yes, sir. I don't want any part of her, sir—"

"You're thinking about my daughter's parts?" .

CHAPTER 19

Returning to Verona High School was not a happy thought for Dennis. Once he was outed as a LARPer, his social life took a nose dive, unparalleled in the history of the school. Mark and Freddy weren't the most popular kids in the school. They'd started off near the bottom, and pretty much stayed there.

Dennis's life was a foregone conclusion. Then it wasn't.

It was almost as if—no, it wasn't almost, it was—true that Dennis could draw a very definitive line between his pre and post-LARP life. That line was drawn the moment he stuck up for Mark in gym class, so many years ago. A single, seemingly insignificant moment from years ago had defined him, for better or for worse.

Dennis wouldn't have thought about it had he left Verona at some point in his life. If he moved to Pittsburgh like—or maybe even with—Alyssa, no one would have known or cared about the one incident in that ninth grade gym class. He would have gone on, lived his life, maybe taken some good-natured teasing from his friends when he visited Verona at Christmas, but that would have been it.

But here he was, going back to Verona High as a LARPer to, ironically, liberate the island.

The school was surrounded by woods, which helped to hide Dennis and his troops until they could evaluate the situation, move in, and overtake the Mongols. Dennis was on a hill, overlooking the school, peering through his binoculars. He scanned the parking lot, the football field, the rooftop, and the soccer field. "I wonder what they plan on doing with everyone in the school. They're really not doing . . . anything," said a team member to Dennis.

"I really don't think they know what to do," Dennis responded, still looking through his binoculars.

"But they have people in the school. You'd think they'd be

moving them somewhere or something."

"Well, thankfully, they haven't. Makes our job easier," Dennis answered. His voice was automatic, emotionless. He was focused, looking through his binoculars. He wanted to get in quickly and get out quickly. Conversation wouldn't help him do that.

Dennis turned to his troops, who were eagerly awaiting their orders.

"All right, looks like we've got about thirty of them down there, and we don't know how many are inside the building. So we're outnumbered. Doesn't matter, though. If we do this right, they'll never know we were there. From what Freddy said, everyone is in the gym and the cafeteria, on the ground floor. The ground floor can be accessed through the parking lot in the back, and there's only about eight of them there. What we're gonna have to do is have half of us go into the school quietly, and the rest of us will battle the eight Mongols guarding the back. Once the people who are inside are set free, they'll come out and help us, but we gotta keep the Mongols on the outside busy until everyone on the inside can come out and help."

The troops began moving, through the woods, to the back of the building. The woods descended into a valley, and on the upper side of the valley was the edge of the parking lot. Dennis and his unit stealthily navigated the woods, and quietly descended the hill. The benefit of growing up in Verona was really paying off. They were less than twenty feet from the Mongols, and the Mongols had no idea they were there.

There was tension in the air, as Dennis looked at the Mongols. They were so nonchalant, just standing there, looking around. Dennis wanted to pick the right moment to strike, because if he chose the wrong moment, there wouldn't be a second shot.

It didn't really look like there was a right moment, though. If anything, waiting too long could get them spotted.

Dennis turned to his troops, who were huddled around him.

"On my command, the eight of you run over there and take them out," he said in a hushed voice. "Keep it quiet. We don't need any of their friends showing up. Once the Mongols are engaged, the rest of you follow me into the school. Draw your weapons when we enter, and expect the worst."

Dennis took a final peek at the Mongols outside the school. He looked over to his troops, and nodded. Eight LARPers drew their weapons, and ran across the parking lot at the surprised Mongols. At first, the Mongols thought the LARPers were a joke and just stood there, puzzled. But as the LARPers, and their weapons got closer, the Mongols drew their weapons and charged the LARPers.

The ferocity of the battle was not diminished by its size. Although it was only eight on eight, those sixteen people were battling for their lives. The clank of metal on metal echoed through the parking lot, and Dennis was worried that the sound would attract more Mongols. Swords were meeting swords, shields were meeting shields, and fists were meeting faces.

The violence was instant, and Dennis tried not to watch too much of it. He and his group had a goal to accomplish. Since the Mongols were occupied, he signaled for his group to head into the building. As they ran into the school, Dennis took one last look over his shoulder, and could see one of the baggers from the Verona Big Bird Grocery Village on top of a Mongol, pummeling him without mercy.

Dennis and his unit entered Verona High. It smelled exactly as it had when he was a student there—a combination of mustiness, humidity, sweat, and hot dogs. Dennis focused on finding the hostages. The lights were out, and the school was dark. The only light came from the windows, and the battery-powered, neon red EXIT signs placed through the hallways.

The school gym and cafeteria were parallel to each other at the end of the long hallway. It was the main hallway of the ground floor, and there were several smaller hallways that ran parallel to the main hallway.

The unit formed a circle, with the LARPers at the back of the group facing backward, so as to protect the rear in case of attack. Dennis led the group down the hallway, aware that the Mongols could launch a sneak attack from any one of the several parallel hallways.

Slowly, the LARPers crept down the hallway, prepared to battle the unknown. They walked as quietly as possible, with short steps, and controlled breathing. It felt like an attack was inevitable, and they were bracing for the initial blow. Every instinct Dennis had told him to run down the hallway and free the hostages, but if he did that it could draw attention. To spoil it now, because of impatience, would be unforgivable.

Dennis was sweating, and he could feel his nostrils flaring. He squeezed Leviathan tight enough to make his right hand numb.

As they approached the first parallel hallway, Dennis silently motioned for the unit to move against the wall. The group did so, as Dennis knelt and peered around the corner. As far as he could see, in the darkness, there was nothing, or no one, to prevent them from moving to the next point in the main hallway.

When the next corridor approached, Dennis followed the same pattern. He motioned for the unit to get close to the wall in single file, while he crouched down at the intersection and peered down the hall.

Again, nothing but darkness, and lonely neon EXIT signs.

Dennis turned to the group, and motioned them forward. As he stood up and took a step, he heard a smack, saw a flash of white light, and was on his back, dazed. There was the sound of heavy boots running up the corridor, and yelling in a language he didn't understand.

The Mongols had found them.

It felt like hours, but it was only a few seconds before he realized what was happening. He shook off the daze, and yelled, "Attack, attack, draw your weapons!!"

The Mongols were already there, swinging wildly with their own weapons. A few LARPers had trouble getting their weapons out of their sheaths, and were instantly leveled by the Mongols. Dennis struggled to his feet, charging into the melee.

Silence didn't matter anymore. The secret was out, the Mongols were there.

[166]

It was then that Sir Den-gar emerged. Dennis hadn't truly been Den-gar for a very long time. Years, in fact. He had been faking it for so long with LARP, that he forgot what it was like to be Den-gar.

Den-gar was as real as Dennis.

The Mongols would pay for this surprise attack. Cowards attack by surprise, and cowards have no place on the battlefield with Den-gar.

Den-gar was focused. His reflexes flowed like water. The blows, the pain, didn't affect him, because victory was the perfect antidote. There must have been fifteen Mongols, but it didn't matter. There was Den-gar, and then there were the Mongols. He wasn't like these unskilled, untrained, dishonorable heathens. Den-gar was a warrior, and he would show them how a warrior fought.

It was chaos, a swirl of weapons, yelling, and noise. The glass trophy cases that lined the hallways were shattered by flying bodies, and the trophies used as weapons. Nothing was sacred, and the conflict was less of a battle, and more of a fight. LARPers ganged up on Mongols, working in teams to render the enemy helpless.

But, suddenly, it ended as quickly as it began.

As Den-gar pounded a Mongol, he heard someone behind him yelling, "Dennis! Dennis! DENNIS!" Two sets of hands grabbed his shoulders, and pulled him off the bloodied Mongol.

"They surrendered, Dennis. They surrendered," said the military team member. His arms were around Dennis, pulling him back. Dennis relaxed his body, and the soldier released him.

As he looked around the darkened hallway, he saw the Mongols, sitting in a line along the hallway. The LARPers, and their military counterparts, stood guard. The dim light from the EXIT signs was enough to illuminate their frightened faces.

Dennis, confused by the surrender said, "But they attacked us, and then . . ."

"And then they saw you pounding the Mongol on the floor over there, and gave up." Dennis looked over, and saw a few LARPers and Mongols attending to Dennis's punching bag.

[167]

"They just quit," said the soldier.

Dennis shook his head in disbelief. It didn't make any sense.

Another soldier chimed in, "I don't really think these guys wanted a battle. They just attacked because they didn't know what else to do."

"Okay, well, just radio and get them outta here, I guess," Dennis said, wiping his brow. "This whole thing is just crazy. I can't believe they quit so easily. I'm heading to the bottom floor."

As Dennis jogged down the hall, through the doors, and down the steps, he couldn't help but wonder who, or what, was behind this bizarre "army". The Mongols had the element of surprise; they could have easily taken the LARPers, or at least put up more of a fight.

Dennis approached the gym door, and pushed on it. It stuck, and he smiled to himself, remembering that the gym door always stuck. As a student, Dennis and his friends would often kick the door open, as hard as they could, just to hear the sound echoing through the gym.

Boom! The door swung open, only this time, Mr. Chieffo, his high school gym teacher, wasn't there to reprimand him for booting the metal door. As Dennis entered the gym, he was astonished at what he saw. All the hostages wore football helmets, and were armed with hockey sticks and baseball bats. They looked at Dennis, as if they were willing to go through him to freedom.

Dennis approached them, with a slight smile, and said, "It's about time you tried to get outta here."

No response.

"Dennis? Is that you?"

When Dennis turned around, a larger man in a football helmet, carrying a bat, made his way from the back of the hostages. He removed his helmet. It was Brad.

"Brad?" Dennis said.

The brothers were now face to face. Brad moved to embrace Dennis, doing so without thinking. Brad's hug, strong and real, brought Dennis back to reality.

They separated, and spoke at the same time.

"What happened?" Brad asked.

"Are you okay?" Dennis blurted.

There was a beat, as the brothers looked each other over.

"What happened to your eye?" Dennis asked, noticing Brad's bloody eye and bruised cheek.

"Nothing, it was just . . ."

"Denny?" a female voice called from the crowd.

It was Alyssa, tired and disheveled. But to Dennis, she was a dream. She ran and embraced him, burying her head in his chest.

As Alyssa slowly backed away, she could tell that Dennis was fixated on Brad's shiner. He was "The Brad". He gave black eyes, he didn't take them.

"He got that defending me," Alyssa said, gently.

Humbly, Brad added, "A few Mongols decided they'd take a shot at Alyssa. But there was no way I was gonna let them mess with your girl, bro. So I caved in a few heads."

"Then they came back with friends," Alyssa finished.

Brad shrugged. "I made my point. Better me than her."

It was all too much. The Mongols, the high school, Brad, Alyssa. She was his girl? Dennis's high school world, his dream, and his reality were a mangled car wreck in the spot where he stood.

"We broke into the gym storage closet about an hour ago," Brad continued. "If ol' Mr. Chieffo knew we busted into his supply closet, he'd kill us! We armed up and were just about to break out. It took forever, 'cause we had to be quiet doing it. As much as I loved high school, there was no way I was gonna spend another minute here. Then you showed up looking like King Arthur on a quest for the Holy Grain or something."

"It's the Holy Grail, Brad." Dennis rolled his eyes. "We better get moving. C'mon, the others are waiting for us down the hall," Dennis continued, suddenly remembering why he was there. Brad, Dennis, and Alyssa signaled for everyone in the gym to follow them, and went to the cafeteria to round up the other hostages.

At the end of the hallway stood the LARP army, along with

the captured Mongols who had ignited the conflict inside the school. The LARPers who had battled and defeated the Mongols outside joined them. Dennis could hear them saying, "Yeah, they just rolled over after a few minutes. Strangest thing."

The hostages and LARPers headed back out to the parking lot to wait for the capture team. Brad stood with his brother.

"So, the LARPers did this?" Brad asked in disbelief.

"Yeah." Dennis nodded, uncomfortably.

"Look, bro, I'm not gonna give you a hard time. I just wanna know what happened. Believe me, as long as I live, you'll never hear me badmouth LARP again. I might even join!" Brad laughed, slapping Dennis on the shoulder good-naturedly. "Who did you convince that you could pull this off?"

"It's a really long story," Dennis answered. "I'll tell you when we get back to the mainland, but, Jen and Mark, believe it or not, got permission for the LARPers to go in and save the island. We have the full support of the US Army and the President. C'mon, we gotta go. We're not done yet."

"Got an extra sword I can use?" Brad asked Dennis, as the brothers walked down the hall. .

CHAPTER 20

When Governor Serling heard the news, he knew what he had to do.

"Mark just radioed and said that the leader of this bunch of wackos—The King, they call him—is holed up at a church on the hilltop of Verona. We have to go up there and get him to surrender peacefully. You're a local. Is there anyone here who can help us talk him down?" the governor asked Melissa Thomas, a Veronaite who was serving in his unit.

"How 'bout Doc Rossi? He's a shrink, the only one in Verona. Maybe he could reprogram this king or something, get him to withdraw?" replied Melissa.

"This Rossi guy, is he on the island with us?" Ed asked, interested in the idea.

"Yeah, he's a semi-retired LARPer. Older guy, in his 60s. But he's over here. I saw him on the dock on the mainland before we left."

"Great idea, Melissa. I'll radio for him to be sent here."

The governor got on his two-way and asked the leaders of each unit to have Doc Rossi sent over. The more he thought about it, the more it made sense to have some sort of professional intervention with The King before employing deadly force. Even though the governor knew Julian Wilkes—the so-called king—from his army days, he wanted as much support as possible.

The Verona invasion was, more or less, one big hostage situation. It was just like those stories where a madman held a building and its residents hostage, and the local law enforcement would send in a negotiator to try to get the madman to release the hostages before the SWAT teams moved in to take care of the problem.

And The King was a problem.

Doc Rossi showed up a few minutes later and saluted

Governor Serling. "Governor, how can I be of assistance?"

"Well, Dr. Rossi, we have a madman running this whole invasion of Verona. I trained him in boot camp many years ago, so we kind of know each other. The Mongols call him The King, but his real name is Julian Wilkes. In my experience as a government official, in dealing with people like this, it's always best to try to peacefully intervene."

"I concur with your assessment, Governor," Rossi replied. Dr. Rossi already knew where this conversation was headed.

"What we'd like for you to do is to accompany me and my troops up to the church to see if we can talk Julian into surrendering. You're really the only one here who can do this. I don't think anyone else here is as qualified to attempt a peaceful intervention."

"I'm all for it, Governor. I will do everything that I can to bring this situation to a peaceful resolution. However, I must ask: What is Plan B?"

The governor's tone became matter-of-fact. "Plan B goes back to the Plan A we had in coming here. If Julian doesn't surrender peacefully, we'll take him and the remaining Mongols by force."

Dr. Rossi nodded, knowingly. From his experience, he believed this situation would not end peacefully, but he had to try.

Within the hour, the governor had briefed his team, and began the journey to St. Joe's Church on Verona's hilltop.

Because St. Joe's was The King's makeshift palace, it would be heavily guarded. That was to be expected. Freddy, Mark, and Jen's units had returned, and they all joined the governor's battalion for this final push to purge the evil from Verona. Dennis and his unit were still making their way back from Verona High.

Unlike every other conflict with the Mongols, the LARPers were going to engage them on a large scale. No hiding in the woods or taking a back road. No trickery. In order for the governor and Dr. Rossi to get into the church, they had to get past the Mongols guarding the outside. There was no way around it.

Maybe earlier in the day, it wouldn't have been a good idea to directly engage the Mongols. At that time, there were too many variables. But now, each victory had erased those variables, one by one.

Mark didn't even bring his Mongolian death worm gear.

Freddy had gone ahead to scout the location so the LARPers would know what to expect. As the LARPers marched up Main Street, right up the hill to the church, Freddy radioed the governor.

"There's a wall of Mongols surrounding the church. There's maybe seventy or eighty of them, and they are well-armed. They look serious, not like the other Mongol groups we've seen today."

"Thanks, Freddy. Where are you?"

"I'm stationed on the roof of the abandoned convent across the street."

"Good. Lay low and hold your position. Meet up with us when we get there."

"Got it. Freddy out."

The governor stopped the march and called the troops around him in a circle.

"I just got word from Freddy that there's approximately eighty Mongols waiting for us at the top of this hill. So far, we've had it pretty easy today, but things are about to get rough. They're up there protecting their king, and probably know we're coming. Expect violence. Expect bloodshed. This is the last obstacle to freedom for this island, and this is what you signed up for. Don't hold back on them because they're not gonna hold back on you. Swing to kill, fight to defeat. And if they send one of ours to the hospital, we send two of theirs to the morgue. Ladies and gentlemen, draw your weapons and prepare for battle."

The governor looked at his troops. Everyone drew their weapons. None of them cast looks of fear.

The LARP army bore down, and climbed the final two blocks uphill to the church. Freddy saw them coming through his binoculars, and climbed down from the roof of the convent.

"Anything you want me to do, Ed?" Freddy asked.

"Yeah, go up there and get their attention," the governor said, cryptically. Freddy smiled, and ran to the top of the hill, facing the church. A team of Mongols spotted him.

"HEY, I'M THE MONGOLIAN DEATH WORM, AND I'VE COME TO DESTROY YOU!" Freddy yelled at the Mongols. Even if few, or none, of them spoke English, they heard him.

"IF YOU DON'T GET OFF OUR ISLAND NOW, WE'LL SEND THE MIGHTY YETI AFTER YOU TO FINISH YOU OFF!"

Within seconds, a group of Mongols charged Freddy. He ran back down the hill, leading the Mongol group directly into a very prepared, heavily-armed group of LARPers. Freddy's unit separated from the group, and met the Mongols head on, while the rest of the LARPers quickly ran the rest of the way up the hill to the church parking lot.

The Mongols in the parking lot could hear the commotion on the hill, and ran to the other side of the building, meeting the LARPers head on. The sound of clashing swords, mallets, shields, and Morningstars filled the air, along with battle cries, in two languages.

The battle was ferocious, unlike anything that Verona had ever seen, or probably would ever see again. Mailmen, Kiss factory workers, school teachers, truck drivers, and bank tellers fought for the island, their home, against an army who didn't expect resistance. Weekend warriors became hardened veterans with every stroke of the sword. If Verona was going to go down—and twenty-four hours ago it looked like it would—these citizens would go down with it.

Unlike LARP, there were no rules in the church parking lot. There's wasn't anything pretty about it, nothing graceful. The battle would never be mistaken for the Art of War, and the splatters of blood made the grass and black tar parking lot look like a Jackson Pollock painting. It was brute force, with Mongols pounding the LARPers mercilessly, making human nails out of them.

In mere minutes, it became clear that The King had kept his best trained, and most dedicated, soldiers at the church. These weren't the same type of soldier who'd "protected" the bank, park, school, and Kiss plant. This group of Mongolians was a highly skilled war machine loyal to The King. They were focused and intent on killing as many Veronaites as possible. The most qualified, best-armed LARP army would have had an uphill battle against The King's royal guard. They saw Verona as their island and the LARPers as invaders.

While the battle roared, the governor, Dr. Rossi, and a small group of armed LARPers snuck into the church. Dr. Rossi attended St. Joe's, so he knew the layout of the church. They boldly walked into the church lobby, through the double doors, into the sanctuary.

The sanctuary was dark, and the brown décor made it darker. At the front of the sanctuary, in a chair on the altar, sat a man in his 40s. He was wearing a purple robe, and his Nordic features surprised the LARPers. He had blond hair, blue eyes, high cheek bones, and was clearly not of Mongolian descent. To his right and left was a line of Mongol warriors. Like trained guard dogs, the Mongolian guards stood poised to attack at The King's command.

"'Allo, Gov'nor," The King cackled to Ed, in a poor faux British accent. "Wot brings you 'round 'ere?"

The LARPers glared at the madman.

"I didn't have my own robe, so I borrowed one from the back," The King said, this time using his real, very educated sounding, accent. "Father-what's-his-name didn't mind. If you don't believe me, you can ask him yourself. He's chained in the basement."

Seeing that the LARPers weren't amused by his comment, The King said, "Okay, let's end this quickly. You tell me that it's over, I'll say that it's not, and then my guards will provide you with a visual that will brilliantly illustrate to you who is, in fact, in charge of this island."

Dr. Rossi stepped forward. "What are you hoping to

[175]

accomplish? How can we aid you in peacefully meeting your goal?"

The King laughed, and replied, "Heeeeey, you're not my shrink. You can't be. I threw him off the boat on the way over here."

Dr. Rossi was taken aback by The King's flippant response.

"'How can we aid you in meeting your goal?'" The King said, mocking Rossi. "Let me tell you how I can help you in meeting my goal," The King said, suddenly turning angry. "My goal is to get you off of my island. If you want to help me reach this goal, stay right where you are. I'll send my guard down to separate your heads from your bodies. Then, I'll roll your heads down the basement steps so that Father-what's-his-name will have someone to talk to. Questions?"

Dr. Rossi gave the governor a look indicating that negotiations would not be successful.

The governor read Rossi's look perfectly, but had another question. "Yeah, I got a question, Julian—"

"You will call me KING!!!! I demand respect from you!!!!" The King pounded his spear on the altar. His disposition shifted, again, and he became friendly. "Hey, Eddie boy! Wow, look at you. Lil' Eddie is the big man on campus. Your folks must be so proud," The King said, with a huge mocking smile. "How've you been? What have you been up to? Let me guess—lying and stealing the tax payers' money, right?

The governor continued, pretending that he hadn't heard The King.

"How does a nut like you con all these people into coming over here? What drove you over the edge to make you do this?"

The King's demeanor flipped again, and he became enraged. He stood up, and pointed at the governor. "I didn't drive over the edge, the edge pushed me over. It was you. You are responsible for this!" The King's hysterical voice echoed through the hallowed sanctuary.

The governor replied in a low, stern voice. "The Julian I knew wasn't a maniac. I have no idea who you are."

"No, but you know me!" The King angrily replied.

[176]

Dr. Rossi could tell that The King was losing his remaining grip on reality.

"There is no negotiating to be done here. He clearly suffers from delusional narcissism disorder, and the only remedy for that is a medication regimen, and years of therapy, which we don't have the luxury of enforcing. I think we should abandon this plan of action, and go with Plan B," Rossi whispered to the governor.

"Let's just wait and see what he says," the governor replied. The King was oblivious to Dr. Rossi and the governor talking about him.

The King walked partially down the aisle. He angrily, mockingly, addressed the governor. "I am every American, Governor, that you spit on every day that you go to work. I'm an American. I was born in Independence, Iowa, right in the middle of nowhere. Nothing but corn, beans, and hogs as far as you can see." The King gestured grandly, as if pointing out an Americana landscape.

He was calm, speaking as if he were reminiscing with an old friend. "I worked hard, got good grades, served in the military, and used the GI Bill to go to the Stern School of Business at NYU. I'm sure you know all about that school, right, Governor? Men of privilege, like yourself, don't earn their way into school." He paused, summoning the necessary feelings to properly convey his message. "Daddy writes a check for them and all of a sudden they're in, like magic! It wasn't magic for me, Eddie, it was work. Good old-fashioned mid-western American work that got me into school!"

"So good for you. You got into school. What's the problem?" the governor asked, defiantly.

"DO NOT INTERRUPT ME WHEN I AM SPEAKING!" The King barked at the governor.

In a mock-composed tone, The King continued, "I graduated Magna Cum Laude from Stern, with a master's degree, no less. I graduated on a Friday and began work at the New York Stock Exchange the following Monday. Within two years, I was making six figures. Within five years, I was making mid-six figures. Had a place on the Upper West Side. Dated a Knicks cheerleader, bought my first Ferrari at the age of 28. And then you know what happened, Governor?"

The governor clearly had had enough of The King's ravings, "She realized you were nuts?"

The King smirked at the governor's comment. In a calm voice, he said,

"No, Governor. The economy collapsed. And so did my life. The job ended, the Ferrari got repossessed, the apartment was foreclosed on, and the girl ran off with the junior mayor. Typical story, right? So I got a job hustling carts at a local grocery store because where else do you work when no one is hiring?" The King was getting wound up again. His anger began to boil over.

"And while I was hustling carts, with my fancy diploma, I got to thinking, why doesn't somebody do something to stop the bleeding? Why doesn't somebody do something to stop the bleeding? Why doesn't somebody do something to stop the bleeding? Over and over and over again, running through my head was that phrase: why doesn't somebody do something to stop the bleeding?" The King pounded himself on the head with his hand as he repeated the phrase. "But nobody—NOBODY— did anything to stop it. Not your government, Governor! Quiz time. What did the government do to stop the country from going bankrupt? Anyone? Anyone? Right! They spent more money! In fact, they gave money away!!! But where was mine?"

"Yours, you spoiled brat, is with everyone else's. It's in freedom of choice, in democracy, in capitalism," the governor shot back.

"Why didn't somebody stand up and do what was right?" The King got quiet. "Because they all did what they wanted. Nobody did what was right; nobody tried to save America as she lay dying. They just pulled the plug and gave up. Nobody did what was right. They just did what they wanted. So, I did what I wanted. I scrimped and saved, and moved to Mongolia. Why Mongolia? Because they're warriors, dedicated to living life the way it's meant to be lived—honestly. And, there is a strong attachment to their history, and a distrust of the government. My beliefs lined up with theirs, and it wasn't hard for me to develop my own . . . following . . . to aid me in rebuilding Eden. We planned this out for years, and our execution was flawless. Like the lazy, fat Americans of the twenty-first century, Verona went like sheep to the slaughter. "

The governor knew what he was dealing with. A maniac, a psycho, a conspiracy theorist. The King wasn't going to listen to logic, let alone anything the governor had to say, but he couldn't resist.

"You're no American, Julian. Americans, don't give up. Americans fight until the bitter end for what they believe in. Americans don't sit around, whine and do nothing. And, the last king who tried to take our land got his royal butt kicked back across the Atlantic."

"YOU CALL THIS NOTHING?!" The King exclaimed, as he pointed to his guards. "THIS is what America is. Overthrowing a corrupt government. Do your homework, Governor, this is how America got started! You're looking at the new George Washington!"

"I'm looking at the new Benedict Arnold." The governor sneered.

"AHHHHHH!!!" The King wailed in anger. "GET OFF MY ISLAND, NOW!" The King had lost all attachment to self-control and reality. He was a raving lunatic.

"You're wrong, King," a voice said from the church lobby. "This isn't your island, it's ours. And it's time you left."

The governor's unit parted, and in walked Dennis, Brad, Freddy, Mark, Joe Peacock, and Jen, all heavily armed.

"Who . . . are . . . you???" The King asked, incredulously.

"I'm Dennis, and I'm here to take the island back, for all the families who have been here for over a hundred years. No one is going to take it from us. No one."

Brad pulled a football helmet from his backpack. As he put his helmet on, he said, "And I'm Brad, the guy who's gonna punt you right off this island!"

Brad got in a football stance, and launched himself at The King.

[179]

"Oh, boy," was all Dennis could get out before he yelled, "ATTACK!"

Just like a real medieval battle, both groups ran right at each other, a pile of shields, weapons, and armor. The sanctity of the church was not recognized, as pews were used for tactical advantage. Tables were overturned, century-old statues used to block fatal blows, and the ancient church organ destroyed. But there was a higher cause here, higher than the symbolism behind each object. The freedom of the island was at the forefront. If the Mongols won, none of the church relics would matter, anyway.

Dennis was exhausted, but he carried on, because this battle was who he was. He was a LARPer from Verona. If he wasn't a real warrior, he wouldn't be here.

He could taste the warm tang of his own blood on his lips, but didn't know where it was coming from. It could have been from his split lip, or his bloody nose. Or maybe from the molar that was now loose in the back of his mouth. You take enough blows to the face and head from an armed, angry Mongol, and that happens. No matter, pain was temporary.

Brad was back in his element. It was the fourth quarter, championship game. Two minutes left, down by a touchdown, and he was in the enemy's zone. This time, his knees weren't going to fail him. And if they did, he would fight on his knees, and, if necessary, on his back. He had never used a sword before today, never even held one. Before today, walking around with a sword was for his dorky little brother, and his weirdo friends.

Today was a different story.

Brad got it. He finally got the feeling of freedom, of accomplishment, from going eye to eye with another man, battling for land or principal.

It was just like high school football. But better, because this victory would last longer, and mean more, than winning a trophy and getting a kiss from the head cheerleader.

Brad had been a LARPer his entire life. He'd just worn a different uniform.

Freddy thought of his ancestors as he battled, and could feel their power and skill surging through his veins. Fighting ability had to be genetic. It had to be. He had never been engaged in a battle like this, and here he was, beating a guy twice his size. He wondered if Mark and Dennis remembered that he always said that he would be a great Mongolian warrior. Of course, he never thought that he would battle his own people. But was he really battling his own people?

No, not at all.

He was battling with his people, against an invader. Freddy wasn't Mongolian any more than Mark was a sorcerer named Vollrath—although he would never say that to Mark. Freddy was an American, born at the same small Verona hospital like everyone else on the island, and the island belonged to him, as much as anyone.

Speaking of Vollrath, he made his presence known at St. Joe's. Even Mark wasn't so far gone that he would try something like the Mongolian death worm in a situation like this. But, he always had something else planned for battle. Because LARP was Mark's life, he was probably the most prepared for this battle. This was the moment he'd dreamed about his entire life. Finally, finally, all the battle research he had done over the years was truly paying off. It had paid off before when the team won a few LARP tournaments, but now it really mattered.

As he threw smoke bombs inside the church to confuse the enemy, and sparks somehow shot out of his sleeves, Mark wondered if all the people who secretly mocked LARP, and him, would finally accept them once Verona was free.

Jen pounded the butt of her sword into the mouth, and down the throat, of a Mongolian. *Bet I just changed his mind about 'the fairer sex'*, she thought, as her Mongol opponent fell to the ground, spitting out a few teeth.

She looked around, and realized she was the only woman in the church.

Jen was willing to bet that the Mongols didn't expect much from her as an opponent in battle, and she was eager to prove them wrong. Like Freddy, war was in her genes. Even though she wasn't a Veronaite, she had something to prove, namely, that

[181]

women and men are equal on the battlefield. This pretender king wanted to take society back to a time when women were thought of as property, and there was no way Jen was going to let that happen.

Plus, she wanted to prove to her dad that "Daddy's little girl" could take care of herself. And a few Mongols, when necessary. Mongols who didn't take her seriously were painfully shown the error of their ways.

Despite his quiet, introspective demeanor, Joe Peacock was a vicious swordsman. He fought with a sword of multicolored metal in each hand, twirling and striking, moving to an unheard rhythm. Mongols were dropping all around him, one after the other, and Joe would simply move on to the next foe. Mark, who was fighting nearby, marveled at Joe's skill, and his multicolored swords.

As Mark shot another lightning bolt out of his sleeve, he heard Joe yell in agony. Mark quickly finished off his opponent, and turned to see Joe, on his knees, a sword protruding from his ribcage. A Mongol stood behind him, with an evil, bloody smile. The Mongol was battered, on his last legs, and Joe probably thought that Mongol was defeated. Somehow, some way, the Mongol managed one final blow.

A fatal blow.

Mark immediately rushed over, snatching one of Joe's swords. Kicking the Mongol in the chest, against the nearest wall, Mark thrust Joe's sword into the Mongol's gut, while simultaneously slitting the Mongol's throat with a dagger. Mark didn't have the time to react to his own actions. He got on his knees, and cradled Joe's head in his arms. Blood was pouring out of Joe's chest, onto his purple vestment.

"Thanks, buddy," Joe whispered.

"We gotta get you outta here," Mark said, panicking.

"No . . . no . . ." Joe coughed "You've gotta finish the job. We didn't come this far to stop."

Mark understood what was happening, but didn't acknowledge it. "I'll call a capture team, and we'll have you out of here in a few minutes, I promise."

Mark looked into Joe's eyes. They were brown, with a hint of red, much like Joe's hair. Mark had looked into those eyes, so many times over the years, treating Joe more like a pawn, than a person.

"I'm sorry, Joe. I never should have . . ."

"It's okay, Mark. It's okay." Joe's voice was fading. He smiled, weakly.

Mark felt a hand on his shoulder. It was Jen, her eyes filling with tears. She had seen Mark go to Joe's aid, and ran to his side, as he gently consoled his friend.

Joe sighed, and then there was nothing.

Mark looked at Jen, his face ashen, his eyes glazed over. A few other LARPers saw what was happening, and rushed over.

"Hide him in the confessional booth in the back." Mark's voice quivered. The LARPers respectfully picked Joe up, and did as they were told.

Jen put her hand on Mark's arm, helped him to his feet, and whispered, "The Mongols are scattering and the capture teams are gathering them up. There's nothing more we can do here." She put her arm around Mark's shoulder and together they exited the church.

The battle was winding down, and the Mongols were strewn throughout the church, some defeated, some dead. Ed spotted The King escaping through a side door, and chased his former protégé, tackling him in the parking lot. Teacher and student rolled around, exchanging blows. The King's years of psychopathic frustration exploded in every punch, rattling the governor's brain. But then the governor would gain the upper hand, unleashing punishing, jackhammer-like punches to The King's jaw and nose.

"Not bad for a government stooge!" The King cackled, as he threw Ed to the ground.

Ed swept The King's leg, and, in one motion, had The King on the ground, in a choke-hold. "This stooge practices Krav Maga to keep in shape," Ed growled into The King's ear.

"So, what are you going to do, Eddie, choke me to death?" The King gasped through his missing teeth. "You'll have blood

[183]

on your hands, like every other government official!"

Although the idea of ending The King's life was incredibly appealing, Ed knew better. "No, you're going to face justice, like the criminal that you are," Ed grunted. He could feel The King's body weakening from a lack of oxygen.

The King reached into his pocket, pulling out a nickel-plated 9mm revolver. "You've forgotten, Eddie. This is my island. I'm in charge. I'll walk before they make me run . . . and you can come, too." The King raised his arm, cocked the gun, and aimed it directly at himself, and Ed.

"You almost won this one, Eddie . . . almost . . ."

It was in slow motion. Ed could see The King squaring the gun at both of them, his bloody finger squeezing the trigger, and he thought he smelled the scent of gunpowder. Milliseconds before the trigger was completely depressed, The King's hand was split by an arrow. The gun fired, the bullet nearly missing Ed's right ear.

The King spit out a blood curdling scream, as Ed heard the pounding of boots on pavement. He released the choke, and his eyes were filled with the vision of Jen, holding a bow. Brad picked up the gun, and held it up for everyone to see. "Can you believe this clown? He has his own people fighting with clubs and swords, and the whole time, he's packin' heat!" Brad looked down at The King, and scolded, "Cheaters never win, your Highness," before tossing the gun into the wooded hills. The King was rolling around in agony, his hand a gushing fountain of blood.

Julian Wilkes, The King, was a writhing, crimson mess, in a royal robe.

"Are you okay, Governor?" Dennis asked, crouching to his knees.

"I'm fine. Fine," Ed said. He was shaken up, covered in cuts and bruises. Ed accepted Freddy's hand and stood up.

Ed gestured to the bow in Jen's hand. "That was an unbelievable shot," he said in amazement.

"Thanks," Jen answered, sheepishly. "I only had one arrow, so it had to count."

The King weakly stood, and tried to get away. Brad instinctively grabbed him by his neck, and dragged him over to the governor.

"When the court system is done with you, you're gonna wish that bullet had made it to your skull," the governor said. "You'll be tried as a traitor and a terrorist. We'll see how well you do with the big boys in a military jail."

"Well, you won't be getting my vote next year, Governor. Not after your behavior today," The King croaked.

Dennis took his radio from his belt. "This is team leader Dennis. Send all available capture teams to St. Joe's. We've got Julian Wilkes. Tell everyone that Verona is free." .

CHAPTER 21

"Has anyone seen Mark?" Freddy asked, as he looked around.

Jen knew this was coming, but had blocked it out. She knew that to win the battle, she had to focus on fighting. Now that the battle for Verona was over, and the island was free, she could deliver the news to the others.

"Listen, guys, I have something to tell you," Jen began, as she quietly recounted the story of Joe Peacock's last minutes, and of Mark's bravery.

Freddy, Brad, Dennis, and Ed looked at each other in disbelief. Dennis and Freddy embraced each other, crying, as Brad put his arms around both of them.

"Where's Mark?" Dennis asked, wiping his eyes.

"He's sitting by himself, under the big tree in the church playground," Jen answered.

The team headed over to the tree, where they saw Mark, staring off into the distance. By this time, the tiny church parking lot was filled with activity. There were LARPers and military personnel everywhere. A few Mongols, still loyal to their king, offered a weak resistance to their capture, and were immediately silenced by the nearest soldier. The capture teams were sorting through the heap of humanity. It was tough to tell who was alive, unconscious, or dead.

As difficult as Mark could be, and often was, he was still their lifelong friend. They sat around him, on the grass, but didn't know what to say. A soft breeze blew, as dust awoke from its slumber.

"This is my fault . . . all of it. This never should have happened. I took things too far. Joe should still be alive. I should have kept my mouth shut, and let the military handle it," Mark said, to no one in particular. He knew they were there, but he couldn't bring himself to look them in their eyes. At Mark's feet was Joe's multicolored sword, its brilliance darkened with dried blood.

"Mark, you didn't make anyone do anything they didn't want to do," Ed said, gently.

"But it was my idea," Mark answered with finality.

Dennis and Freddy looked at each other. They had never seen Mark so devastated.

"Joe was incredibly brave, and a team player in the best sense of the word," Dennis said. "He came here to help us. Without him rounding up everyone, we wouldn't have been able to do this." Mark's expression didn't change. He was stone-faced, yet there was deep remorse in his eyes. Dennis continued, "What I'm saying is . . . Joe's death wasn't an accident. He was a smart guy, and he knew what he was doing. You didn't cause Joe's death. The Mongols did. Julian Wilkes did. And he'll pay for it"

"I just never treated him . . . or any of you . . . the way I should have," Mark said. He was now focused on the group.

"But you were there for Joe when he needed you the most," Jen chimed in. "Just like you would do for any of us."

"And that's what true friendship is—knowing that you can count on the other person, in any situation," Freddy added. "In that respect, you were Joe's friend."

Mark's countenance softened and he nodded.

"I'm really proud of you, man, and I'm proud to be your friend," Dennis said. "You really showed who you are today. I've spent so much time wishing I was anywhere but here, but now, there's nowhere else I'd rather be. This is my home, and all of you are my family."

"Even me, bro?" Brad asked, trying to lighten the mood.

"Unfortunately, yes," Dennis responded, in mock disgust.

* * *

Verona was free, but a disaster.

Although the damage wasn't irreversible, it would take a long time, and a lot of money, to get Verona up and running again. Right now, the only way to get to Verona was by boat. If nothing else, the Hulton Bridge had to be quickly repaired, so that aid could arrive to the island.

The LARPers, running on the adrenaline of freedom, boarded landing crafts, and headed to the mainland. They would stay in nearby Oakmont, at the Oakmont Inn, which is where the US Army had established a headquarters. Jeeps transported the LARPers back to the inn.

Medical personnel were on hand to treat the LARPers injuries. There were broken bones, chipped and missing teeth, and lots of cuts. Yet, each injury was worn as a badge of honor. Stories were exchanged, pictures taken, and tales were exaggerated. Just like after a LARP tournament.

After getting their medical treatment, Freddy and Mark went to their shared room, Jen to her room, and Brad and Dennis to their room. None of them wanted to discuss the day, not even Mark, who usually rehashed every swing of the sword after a LARP tournament. But not tonight. Tonight was meant for rest, decompression, and mourning the loss of their friend.

Local stores had contributed clothing for the LARPers. Brad changed his soiled, stained clothes, but Dennis was frozen in time, looking down at his bloodied mesh armor.

"You okay, bro?" Brad asked.

"Yeah," Dennis replied, unsure of his own answer.

Brad knew that his brother was hurting, confused at his own actions.

Brad put his hands on Dennis's shoulders, looked him square in the eye, and said, "Listen, Dennis, you did the right thing."

"I killed a few of them today," Dennis said, in disbelief. The reality of the last twenty-four hours was finally attaching itself to his consciousness. "I'm looking at myself, and I don't even feel like me."

"What you did was brave, man," Brad said, comfortingly "Heroes do what nobody else can do. What nobody else will do. You saved me, and lots of other people. I couldn't be more proud to be your brother than I am right now. And . . . I'm sorry . . . sorry that I gave you such a hard time."

Dennis took it all in. He finally heard the words he had longed to hear for so many years. Brad was proud of him.

And he was proud of Brad.

Dennis nodded and hugged his brother.

"Let me know when the next LARP ceremony happens. I want in," Brad said, as if he had just found his true calling.

"We don't . . . have . . . ceremonies," Dennis bristled, his voice tense. He looked Brad dead in the eye, and realized that Brad had spoken out of ignorance, not belittling. Dennis changed his tone. "Look, all you gotta do is sign up with Mark."

Brad nodded and Dennis began undressing, peeling the sweaty clothes off his battered body. He was covered in cuts and bruises, a scrapbook of battle, even though he didn't remember receiving any of the injuries. Brad studied Dennis, worried that the injuries would depress him.

Dennis examined himself, silently, and then looked up at Brad. "You oughta see the other guy," he said with a smile.

Brad laughed, and showed him a scar on his ribcage, left side. "Oh yeah? Take a look at this. Got this beauty junior year. Thirty-yard line versus Oakmont. Dude used me for a trampoline. Of course, on the next play, we ended up in the end zone."

Dennis laughed at Brad. This conversation was going to familiar territory, but one that Dennis was now comfortable with. "Okay, I'm gonna grab a shower now before the Brad time machine fires up and takes us back to high school," Dennis said with a laugh. Brad grinned, acknowledging his stereotype.

* * *

The next morning, long before either Dennis or Brad planned on waking up, there was a quiet knock at their door. They were in a deep sleep, dreaming of going back home, for good. Dennis rolled over, hoping to see Brad getting out of bed to answer the door. Instead, Brad was in a dead sleep, snoring, with his mouth open. Dennis winced as he sat up, and staggered to the door.

He opened the door, and thought he was dreaming.

[189]

It was Alyssa.

"Hi!" she said, with a huge, welcoming smile.

Dennis stared at her for what felt like an eternity. He didn't know what to say, or if this was even happening.

Alyssa, a bit concerned said, "Dennis . . . it's me, Alyssa."

"Hi," Dennis greeted, surprised.

Suddenly, Dennis realized he was standing in the doorway, with his dream girl, in his boxer shorts. Panicked at his near nakedness, he came to life. "Wait here." He returned as quickly as he disappeared, dressed in the mismatched free clothes he got the night before.

"Sorry about that, I was um . . ." Dennis chuckled as he tucked in his shirt.

"Naked?" Alyssa giggled. Her laugh was as invigorating as it was in high school.

"Just about," Dennis said, as they both laughed. "Let's go downstairs and get some coffee. I could use it."

"Sounds great." Alyssa smiled.

As they walked to the elevator, Dennis still couldn't believe Alyssa had knocked on his door. Dennis had thought about Alyssa over the years, but he really didn't think too much about her during the invasion. He was more concerned with saving the island. When he saw her in the gym, he figured that would be it. A "thank you" hug, then back to Pittsburgh.

After getting coffee and a few stale bagels, they found a corner table and sat down, Dennis grunting in pain as he maneuvered across the booth.

"Are you okay?" Alyssa asked, her face scrunched up, reflecting Dennis's pain.

"I don't know," Dennis said groaning. He was trying to be funny, to put her at ease.

"I really can't believe all that you did yesterday."

"Nothing anyone else wouldn't have done under the same circumstances," Dennis replied, humbly.

"'Nothing anyone else wouldn't have done'? Are you kidding? You saved a lot of people yesterday, including your brother. I'd love to do a story on you."

[190]

Dennis paused, his mood changed. "So this is a professional visit, then?"

It was Alyssa's turn to pause. Dennis's comments cut through her, but she tried not to show the depth of the wound.

"No, it's not a 'professional visit'. I came to see you, to check on you. I know you, Dennis. Even though it's been a long time, I know you. And I'm sure that yesterday was pretty rough on you. I wanted to make sure that you were okay."

Dennis took a mental step back, his mood somber. "It was rough. It was. But it had to be done."

"'It had to be done'," Alyssa said, reaching out and grasping Dennis's hand. "But it was you who stepped up and did the right thing."

Dennis nodded in agreement. He wanted to shift the focus of the conversation. "So where were you during the whole thing? An invasion is a pretty rotten welcome home gift, isn't it?"

Alyssa rolled her eyes "Yeah, no kidding. I was at the Rivertowne when they showed up. It was right after I got off the phone with you. I was there with Brad, remember?"

"Yeah," Dennis said, trying not to remember.

Alyssa didn't pick up on Dennis's tone, and continued her story.

"We were just sitting there, having a Rivertowne Brew, listening to Brad go through his greatest hits of football stories, when the Mongols rushed the place and started dragging everyone out. They didn't say anything. They just came and dragged us out. Some of the people tried to fight back, including your brother. But they knocked him out, and a few others, which showed the rest of us what would happen if we tried to fight back."

Dennis had to ask the million-dollar question. Or, more accurately, the life-changing question. "So, um, before the Mongols came in, you were with Brad?"

"Uh huh. Don't you remember? I talked to you on the phone."

"Yeah, yeah. But, um, what did you do after we hung up?"

"What do you mean?"

"Well, right after you gave the phone back to Brad, when I said that I couldn't come to the Rivertowne to see you, he said . . ."

"He's been saying that for years." She shook her head, dismissively. "Brad's more like an older brother to me. Nothing happened that day. Or ever, for that matter."

Dennis, relieved at her answer, pushed the envelope a little further. "So, if Brad is your older brother, does that make me . . . ?"

Alyssa saw where the conversation was going, and was happy to play along. "Brad's dorky younger brother!"

Dennis laughed and shook his head. Some things never change.

Alyssa laughed too. It was like they were in high school again. They were doing the same mating dance, with the same awkward moves. They were gawky teenagers again.

"Actually, I just got off the phone with my producer back in Pittsburgh. He wants me to work on a documentary about Verona, and the invasion. They're gonna try and syndicate it all over the country. So, I took an extended leave of absence from work. Sort of a work/holiday thing."

"Really!" Dennis exclaimed.

"Yep. This is a once in a lifetime—hopefully—Pulitzer situation. So I'm going to be here for a while, staying with my parents, while I work on the documentary."

Alyssa's words brought him the first real happiness he felt, inside and out, for a long time.

"I hope we can spend some time together while I'm here," Alyssa teased, already knowing the answer.

"Well, I'll see if I can schedule you in. I'm pretty busy you know, being a hero and all," Dennis joked.

"You better make time for me," Alyssa said, playfully throwing a rolled-up napkin.

As the two laughed at the joy of the future, Brad made his way to their table.

"Morning, you two," Brad said. He was different than even a few days ago. The Ego was gone.

"How's 'The Brad' doing this morning?" Dennis asked.

Brad smiled at how ridiculous, and unfamiliar, his famous nickname felt to him. "I'm sore all over. I feel like I'm ninety-nine years old. I gotta get back in shape. My body's not used to pounding bad guys."

"Well, the next big LARP tournament is in two months. Better start hitting the gym," Dennis remarked.

Brad was drinking orange juice, and gave Dennis a thumbs up.

Alyssa was shocked. "'The Brad' is going to be a LARPer? What kind of bizarro Verona universe is this? Am I in the Twilight Zone or something?"

Brad was serious. "No, no I'm totally into it. After what those guys and girls did yesterday, how can anyone knock it?"

"Again," Alyssa observed, "bizarro."

"So this is our victory dinner. Or breakfast, I guess," said Freddy, as he pulled up a chair. Mark and Jen were with him.

Mark stood on his chair, and raised a triumphant fist. "VICTORY!" he proclaimed. Instead of the usual annoyance that the group felt toward Mark's public love for LARP, they joined him in his cheer.

"VICTORY!" the rest of the table proclaimed.

As they exchanged morning greetings, it occurred to them that there was an unfamiliar face in the group. It wasn't Alyssa. It was Brad. He could tell they felt a little uncomfortable in his presence, and, quite frankly, after years of ridicule, he didn't blame them.

"Hey, I just want to thank all of you for what you did yesterday. I know I've given you a hard time in the past, but I just didn't know what the whole LARP thing was about. So I just . . . just really appreciate what you did," Brad confessed, diffusing the situation.

Mark, Dennis, and Freddy had been friends for so long that they could read each other's minds, and they all agreed that Brad was genuine, and should be accepted.

Brad addressed Mark, "And, uh, I wanted to ask you if I could train with you guys. Maybe help you out in a few tournaments. Is there room on your team for an old jock?"

"No," Mark replied. "We don't have any room for washed-up jocks."

The table was silent.

"But," Mark continued, "We do have room for 'The Brad', the greatest athlete in the history of Verona High!" he said with a smile.

The people at the table laughed, as Mark and Brad clanked their coffee mugs together.

"So, Alyssa, it's great seeing you again," Freddy affirmed.

"Yeah, it's good to be back. This is definitely a trip home I'll never forget."

"How long will you be here?" Jen asked.

"Don't know. I'm making a documentary about the invasion."

Mark's interest was piqued. "Documentary, huh? Well, you know, Alyssa, I am the leading expert on LARP on the island of Verona, and I did lead the effort for LARP involvement in the invasion. Time permitting, I would be more than willing to donate my expertise to your project. I'm sure you'll find me an invaluable resource."

"I'll keep that in mind," Alyssa answered, in a faux dismissive tone.

"Hey, don't spend too much time being a hero. I still need you to be . . . whatever it is that you are," Jen remarked, elbowing Mark in the ribs. Everyone at the table gave each other a puzzled look. Jen was acknowledging Mark's presence? Without assaulting his ego?

Jen picked up on the vibe, and looked at the group. "Don't question it," she acknowledged, with a smile.

"Yes, please don't," Mark ordered, as the table erupted in laughter.

As Dennis shook his head in disbelief, he felt a hand on his shoulder.

"Good morning." It was Governor Serling, with General Cassady.

After everyone exchanged greetings, General Cassady

asked, "Everyone okay today?" The group looked around the table, checking on each other, as they nodded.

The general continued. "Good, glad to hear it. Dennis, Freddy, Mark, and Jen, would you please come with us?" The four friends excused themselves from the table, and followed Ed and General Cassady.

They were led to a conference room at the inn. Men in black suits, with black sunglasses and ear pieces, lined the hallway.

In the small conference room sat the President of the United States. He rose from his chair, and extended his hand. "Hello, I'm President Vianisi. It's an honor to meet you."

Freddy, Jen, Mark, and Dennis didn't know what to do. The president was used to this response, and played it off.

"Don't worry, I won't hurt you," the president cracked. "After what you did to those terrorists yesterday, I don't think that I could!" The president's humor helped to ease the tension, and, after introductions were made, everyone sat at the round conference table.

"Your country is very proud of you. All of you stepped up to the plate, and knocked it out of the park. I'm sure it was difficult, and you probably saw things that you never saw before, and didn't want to see. But you did it not only for your own good, but for the benefit of the country. All of you sent a strong message to the rest of the world that Americans will defend their land, no matter the cost. To commemorate your brave work, one week from today will be National LARP Day. We're planning a huge parade and celebration in Washington, and everyone in attendance will be encouraged to dress up as a character, either real or imagined. I hope you'll be able to attend the celebration."

Mark, Dennis, Jen, and Freddy were speechless. "I think that's a 'yes', Mr. President," General Cassady said.

"Good," the president said, with a broad smile. "The nation is eternally grateful for your service, and we look forward to celebrating your victory."

Dennis finally spoke.

"Mr. President, this is just . . . I don't know what to say. I'm just some guy from a tiny island nobody ever heard of. This time last week I was sitting in my cube, wondering if my life was ever going to get any better. And now—"

"It has," the president said, finishing the sentence.

Dennis hesitated, thinking of everything he'd experienced. "Well," he continued, "it's definitely heading there."

Mark got the courage to speak. "Well, Mr. President, we're certainly appreciative of your offer. As the leading LARP expert in the greater Northwest region, my services are available to the nation, as a celebratory consultant or military strategist, anytime you may need assistance."

"The nation thanks you," the president replied, in a sort of mock solemn tone.

"Uh, Mr. President, I have a question," Jen said.

"Sure, go right ahead," the president responded, engagingly.

"What's going to happen to the Mongols who invaded the island?"

The president thought for a moment. "Well, Jen, quite honestly, I'm not sure. They did attempt a hostile takeover of American soil, and they did succeed in that take over for a short time. They committed a terrorist act, so we're going to have to treat them the way we would any terrorist."

"With all due respect, Mr. President, I need to give you some information, which will hopefully make you reconsider," Jen disclosed.

The president looked intrigued, and General Cassady spoke up.

"Jen, I think you're out of your element here. This is really the president's call, not yours."

"No, it's okay, General, I'm interested in hearing what she has to say. G'head, Jen," the president said, kindly.

"Well, sir, my unit was in charge of liberating the hostages that were held at the Verona bank. As we saw throughout the retaking of the island, more often than not, the Mongols offered very little resistance. They didn't really guard the hostages very well, and did virtually nothing to guard or protect their land."

"Go on," urged the president, intently listening to Jen's every word.

"When we took the bank, the Mongols didn't really fight back at all. Our side just cut right through them. There weren't even any guards in the bank. And then, I met Inga in the basement of the bank. She emigrated from Germany, and has lived in Verona for forty years. While she was locked up in the bank's cellar, she spoke to the Mongols who fed the hostages. Inga was convinced that the majority of the Mongols were just looking for a better opportunity in America, and The King provided them with the means to get it. They really didn't know what it entailed, not really. The Mongols weren't here to cause strife. They just wanted out of where they were. When Inga told me what she learned from speaking to, and observing, the Mongols, I thought there was something wrong with her, but the more she spoke, the more it made sense. The Mongols weren't a militant group, at least not all of them. They were immigrants, just like my ancestors were, and your ancestors. Granted, they went about it the wrong way, but still, isn't America all about giving someone a chance at a better life?"

The president continued to listen. Jen could tell that her message was being heard. She continued, "The King, and his guard, they were a different story. You could tell by the way they fought. But, the rest of them . . . they just fell for the words of a madman. I think they were just as surprised at what was happening as we were. I'm just asking, Mr. President, that you please give careful consideration to the resolution of this situation. Like a lot of things in life, sir, this isn't what it first appeared to be."

President Vianisi nodded in agreement. "Thank you for the information, Jen. I promise I'll consider it." Jen smiled, and nodded. President Vianisi continued, "I thank you for your time. I'm going to go to Verona now and look things over. I'll see you in Washington next week." Standing up, the president shook hands with everyone in the room.

Freddy, Mark, Dennis, and Jen walked back to their table, star struck from meeting President Vianisi.

"So what happened?" Brad asked, anxiously.

"Met the president," Dennis said matter-of-factly.

[197]

"What?" Alyssa asked.

"Yeah, the president," Freddy acknowledged, in the same tone. They sat down to finish their coffee.

"Well, c'mon tell us!" Brad begged.

Dennis stopped the ruse, and recounted the whole meeting to Brad and Alyssa. As they did, the president, and his security detail, walked past them and waved.

"See you next week." President Vianisi waved, cheerfully.

"Take care, sir," Freddy responded.

"That is definitely going in the documentary," Alyssa said. .

EPILOGUE

Sir Den-gar stood on the terrace of his castle, proudly surveying his kingdom. It was a year to the day that he spilled his blood on the green pastures of Verona, battling for its independence. He felt closer to his kingdom than ever before. His heart beat for Verona.

The restored, thriving Verona was the epitome of peace and prosperity. The legend of Den-gar's heroics, and those of his allies, spread throughout the land. People the world over knew that Verona had encountered a great evil, and conquered it.

The world celebrated Den-gar's name, and Den-gar knew that his life, and the life of all those in his kingdom, would continue to be blessed.

And Den-gar would continue to ensure the peace of Verona.

Den-gar left the terrace, and went to his courtyard. He drew his legendary sword, the mighty Leviathan, and studied it in the brilliant morning sunlight. Leviathan was old, every scratch and knick on its blade a tale of victory. Despite its age, Leviathan was still mighty, still strong, still feared.

And still beautiful.

This was the blade that had helped to earn peace for Verona.

This was the blade that had helped to win the battle for Verona.

Today was the first ever Freedom Day celebration in Verona. Den-gar, and the rest of the Hotzenbella Kingdom, would play a big part in the celebration.

As Den-gar was polishing Leviathan, preparing the weapon for a demonstration later in the day, he heard Lady Alyssa's voice.

"Denny? Phone. It's Brad."

Dennis smiled. This time last year, the mere mention of Brad's name would have elicited a sick feeling in Dennis's gut.

But not this year.

"Hey, bro, what's going on? You ready to hit the Outlook Woods and beat South Hills?" Brad inquired, happily.

"Yep, I can't wait. Just getting Leviathan ready for today. You?"

"Just gettin' my gear on. The Mongols there yet?" Brad asked.

"No, haven't heard from Mark. They're going to his house, and we're all going to leave from there."

"Okay, cool," Brad said. "Are we still going with the same scenario that we discussed last weekend?"

"Yep, far as I know. Unless Mark has changed it, which is a very real possibility. Wait, hold on, that's Mark on the other line." Dennis pushed his call waiting button.

"Hey, you ready to go? I got a group of angry Mongols here who are itchin' to beat up on the South Hills LARPers," Mark said. Dennis could hear a group of people in the background.

"Okay, I got Brad on the other line. We'll be over in fifteen minutes."

"Better make it ten. Chuluun and Sükh want to hit the buffet line before the competition. And Oyunbileg needs your help in repairing her axe. She broke it last week," Mark replied.

"Okay, we'll be there in ten," Dennis said, pressing the call waiting button to return to Brad. "Hey, I'll be there in five minutes, be ready. The Mongols are there, but they need to hit the buffet first, and we gotta do some weapon repair."

"Good deal, see you then," Brad answered, excitement in his voice.

Dennis hung up the phone, and turned to Alyssa. "Who would have thought, huh?" he asked, as he kissed her forehead.

"Not in my wildest dreams," she replied, nuzzling into his chest. "I'm so glad I left Pittsburgh to come back home. I probably never should have left."

"But if you wouldn't have left, we might never have . . . connected. I guess in a weird way, the invasion brought us together."

Alyssa giggled. "Make sure you thank the Mongols today when you see them."

"I think we thanked them enough with all the wine they drank at our wedding," Dennis said, sarcastically. "I still have the awful sound of Sukhbataar and Doc Rossi's drunken duet of 'Gloria' ringing in my ears."

"I didn't think it was ever going to end," Alyssa added, smiling at the memory of their wedding earlier in the year.

"I can't believe Jen was able to talk President Vianisi into letting the innocent Mongols go. I mean, she was right. After getting to know them this past year, it's pretty clear that they were just looking for a new opportunity. But still . . ."

"You don't think anything will happen to them at the documentary premiere, do you?" Alyssa asked, a little scared by the thought.

"Naw, they'll be all right. In the last year, they've really acclimated themselves to our culture. They love it here in Verona, and from what I've seen, Verona loves them," Dennis replied, confidently.

"I hope they'll be okay. I don't want the documentary to bring up any bad memories."

"It'll be fine," Dennis reassured. "The Mongols have gone all out for this. They got tuxes, nice dresses, everything. They're all very excited. Everyone here knows that the ones who meant to harm us are now locked away for a long time, very far away from here. The ones who stayed here are just as much a part of Verona as I am."

Alyssa nodded, agreeing with Dennis. "I never thought when we were kids that I'd have a movie playing at the Oaks. All the thousands of times we've been there, and now we're the stars! It was really nice of the network to have the world premiere here."

"LARP: The Battle for Verona," Dennis teased, sounding like a movie-voiceover announcer. "Four lifelong friends struggle to free their homeland from the clutches of an evil madman. The feel good documentary of the year! In theaters now!"

"I just hope Mark doesn't get angry at the way he comes off in the film," Alyssa added, a bit concerned. "But I tried really hard not to make him seem like . . . himself."

[201]

"He'll be fine," Dennis said with a chuckle. "I'm sure he'll be happy just seeing his face on a forty-foot screen. He can add 'movie star' to his bottomless pit of really bad pickup lines. Between the movie and his gig tonight with Camelot, I'm sure today will feed his ego for the next twenty years. You did a great job on it. I'm sure everyone will love it."

Dennis placed his hand on Alyssa's stomach. "I think I just felt him kick."

"Yeah, you did," she replied, resting her hand on his.

"Looks like little Brad is gonna be a great football player, like his uncle," Dennis suggested.

"Or a great warrior, like his father," Alyssa hinted, looking up at Dennis.

"I hope so. I can't be out there swinging Leviathan forever. Somebody's gotta take over."

"Well, you'd better go," Alyssa said, kissing Dennis. "You don't want to keep the Mongols waiting. You know how Odval gets when you're late."

"Don't remind me," Dennis echoed, in mock worry. "See you at St. Joe's tonight for the fireworks, then the premiere, right?"

"We'll be there," Alyssa confirmed, referring to her and little Brad. "And, hey, you better beat South Hills. Today is a celebration of your victory, so you better have your 'A' game. Don't let me down, Den-gar!"

"Not for the world, my beloved Lady," Dennis avowed, kneeling to Alyssa.

Dennis exited the courtyard of their home, and shouted from the driveway. "VICTORY!"

"VICTORY!" Alyssa shouted back, as little Brad kicked inside of her.

ABOUT THE AUTHOR

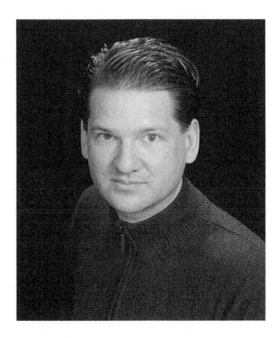

Justin Calderone started writing books when he was old enough to hold a pencil. He pursued writing professionally after reading Jack Kerouac's *Desolation Angels*. His first book, the poetry novel *Revolutions*, was published in 2004.

Twitter @justincalderone

Made in the USA
Monee, IL
10 January 2021